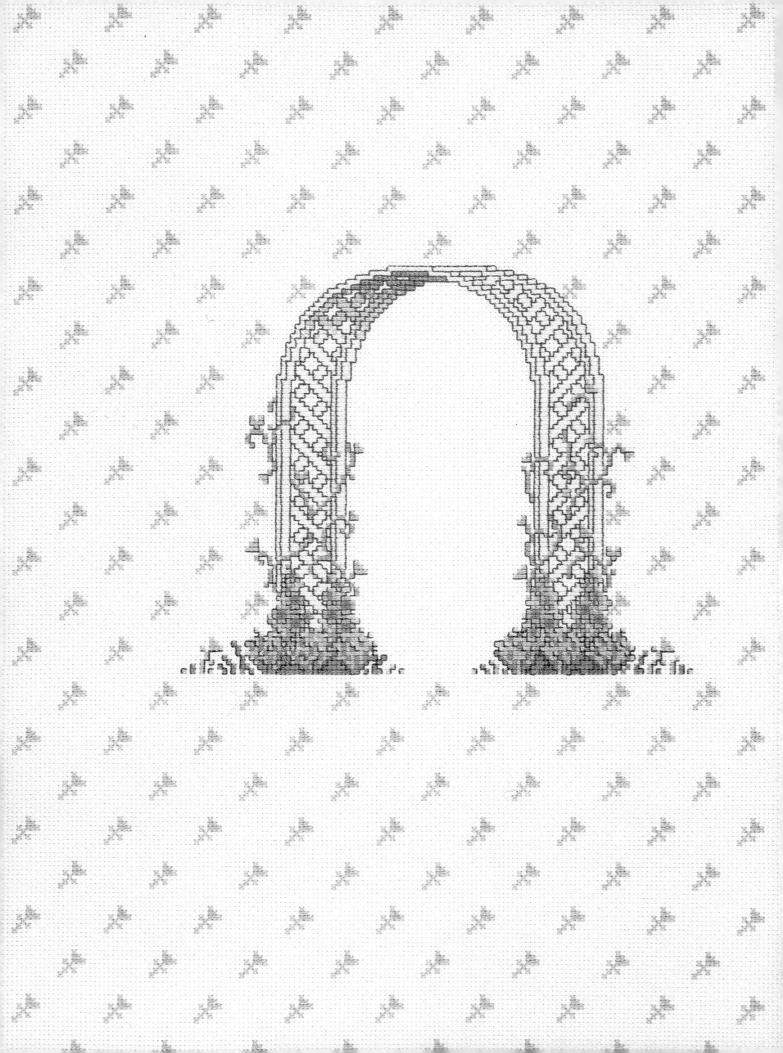

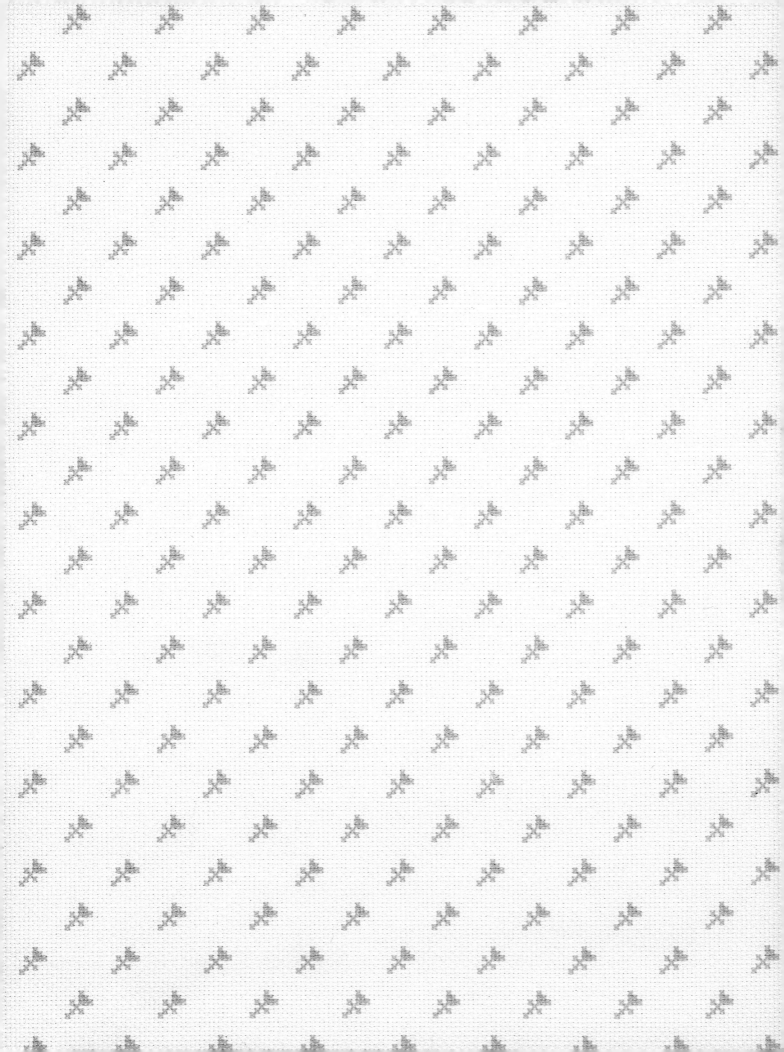

CROSS-STITCH PATTERNS
for

MOTHER GOOSE'S WORDS OF WIT AND WISDOM

Samplers to Stitch

TEDD ARNOLD

E.P. DUTTON / DIAL BOOKS   NEW YORK

Dedicated to Gerry Schultz whose work was the seed from which an idea grew, and to my wife Carol who nurtured, weeded, trimmed, loved, and brought this book to fruition.

Acknowledgments
Many hands pulled miles and miles of thread through what seemed to be acres of cloth to produce this book. My heartfelt thanks to all who gave of their time and kept me in stitches:

Ursula M. Paccone	Sharon J. Newman	Mary Jane Rolls	Susan H. Arnold
Pam Grant	Ruth Elizabeth Bruning	Marcia H. Robinson	Netti Caporiccio
Carol Arnold	Lisa Hilliard	Cheri A. McElroy	Marie K. Dale
Pat Batulis	Laura L. Palmer	Debbie Reynolds	Janet I. Pierotti
Geraldine Schultz	Cathy Clark Harrell	Pat Reimsnyder	Anne E. Marshall
Theodosia R. Schultz	Kay Leininger	Jennifer T. Long	Judith D. Gulick
Debra Haldeman	Margaret Brennan	Deborah M. Spezialetti	Jane Sugawara
Vicki I. Bennett	Reges J. Bush	Denise K. Hagan	Eileen Warren
Frances Padgett	Bob Schultz	Jackie Yacubic	Ann-Marie Allaire
Judy Clark	Patricia M. Bottcher	Maria D. Russ	Eileen N. Hogan
Nancy A. Doman	Mary Jane Buchanan	Mary E. Hildreth	W. Richard Hamlin, Ph.D.
Victoria Rounds	Carolyn S. Winslow	Kelly Pickering	Susannah K. Murphy
Debbie A. Jacobus	Nancy H. Paddock	Sandra A. Clemons	Debra L. Arnold

I'd also like to thank Peter Elek for his unflagging professional support and personal friendship.
Special thanks to Our House Fabric and Gifts, Elmira, New York.
And a tip of the hat to Linda Peterson.
Sewing by Debbie A. Jacobus, Elma Berbary, and Linda Stewart.
Framing by Allen Crittenden Smith of The Art Shop, Horseheads, New York.
Silk arrangement and wreath from Silks By Jan, Elmira, New York.
Antique Googlie doll, surrey, and long paw teddy bear courtesy of Pamela Farr Smith.
Child's rocker courtesy of Diana Warham.
Crib quilt and crocheted table cover by Theodosia Schultz.
Various items courtesy of Betty Kelsey.
Calico goose by Florence Bruning.
Bunny doll by Betty Bower.
Grateful acknowledgment to Betty Ring for providing a photograph of a sampler from her collection.
Grateful acknowledgment to The Pilgrim Society, Plymouth, Massachusetts, for providing a photograph of a sampler from their collection. Photographer: Alan Harvey.
Border linen courtesy of International Linen, New York, New York.

Publisher: Phyllis J. Fogelman
Editor: Toby Sherry
Art Director: Atha Tehon
Designer: Nancy R. Leo
Production Director: Shari Lichtner
Photographer: Lee A. Melen, Northlight Photographic Studios, Ithaca, New York.

Published by E. P. Dutton/Dial Books
A Division of Penguin Books USA Inc.
375 Hudson Street
New York, New York 10014

Library of Congress Cataloging in Publication Data

Arnold, Tedd.
Cross-stitch patterns from Mother Goose's
words of wit and wisdom:
samplers to stitch / Tedd Arnold.
p. cm.
ISBN 0-525-24895-1
1. Cross-stitch—Patterns. 2. Samplers.
I. Mother Goose. II. Title.
TT778.C76A83 1990 746.3'041—dc20 90-3261 CIP

JANUARY

January brings the snow,
Makes our feet and fingers glow.

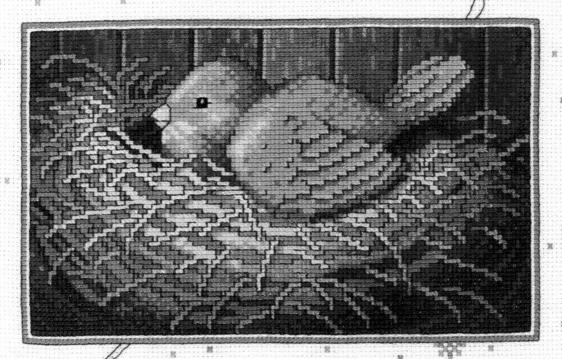

The north wind doth blow,
And we shall have snow,
And what will the poor robin do then?
Poor thing.

He'll sit in a barn,
And keep himself warm,
And hide his head under his wing,
Poor thing.

Whether it's cold, or whether it's hot,
There's going to be weather, whether or not.

The greedy man
Is he who sits
And bites bits
Out of plates,

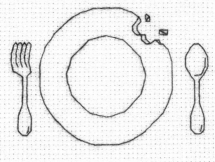

Or else takes up
An almanac
And gobbles
All the dates.

I saw three ships come sailing by,
 Come sailing by, come sailing by,
I saw three ships come sailing by,
 On New Year's Day in the morning.

And what do you think was in them then,
 Was in them then, was in them then?
And what do you think was in them then?
 On New Year's Day in the morning?

Three pretty girls were in them then,
 Were in them then, were in them then,
Three pretty girls were in them then,
 On New Year's Day in the morning.

One could whistle, and one could sing,
 And one could play the violin;
Such joy there was at my wedding,
 On New Year's Day in the morning.

How many days has my baby to play?

Saturday, Sunday, Monday,

Tuesday, Wednesday, Thursday, Friday,

Saturday, Sunday, Monday.

February brings the rain,
Thaws the frozen lake again.

Lavender blue and rosemary green,
When I am king, you shall be queen.

Yankee Doodle went to town,
Riding on a pony.
Stuck a feather in his hat
And called it macaroni.

When Jack's a very good boy,
He shall have cakes and custard;
But when he does nothing but cry,
He shall have nothing but mustard.

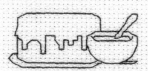

Hey diddle, diddle, the cat and the fiddle,
The cow jumped over the moon.
The little dog laughed to see such sport
And the dish ran away with the spoon.

March brings breezes, loud and shrill,
To stir the dancing daffodil.

One leaf for fame, one leaf for wealth,
One for a faithful lover,
And one leaf to bring glorious health,
Are all in a four-leaf clover.

Sing a song of sixpence,
A pocket full of rye;
Four and twenty blackbirds
Baked in a pie.

When the pie was opened,
The birds began to sing;
Was not that a dainty dish
To set before the king?

There was a crooked man, and he walked a crooked mile,
He found a crooked sixpence against a crooked stile;
He bought a crooked cat, which caught a crooked mouse,
And they all lived together in a little crooked house.

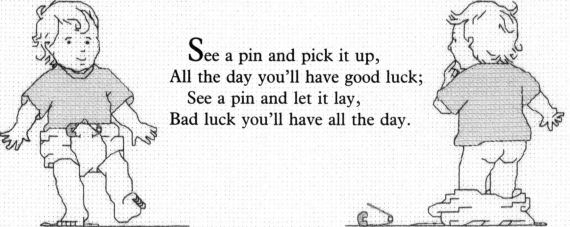

See a pin and pick it up,
All the day you'll have good luck;
See a pin and let it lay,
Bad luck you'll have all the day.

Daffy-down-dilly has
come to town
In a yellow petticoat
and a green gown.

APRIL

April brings the primrose sweet,
Scatters daisies at our feet.

I bought a dozen new-laid eggs,
Of good old farmer Dickens;
I hobbled home upon two legs,
And found them full of chickens.

Rain, rain, go away,
Come again another day.

Baby and I
Were baked in a pie,
The gravy was wonderful hot.
We had nothing to pay
To the baker that day,
And so we crept out of the pot.

Cackle, cackle, Mother Goose,
Have you any feathers loose?
Truly have I, pretty fellow,
Half enough to fill a pillow.
Here are quills, take one or two,
And down to make a bed for you.

May brings flocks of pretty lambs,
Skipping by their fleecy dams.

One, he loves; two, he loves;
Three, he loves, they say;
Four, he loves with all his heart;
Five, he casts away.
Six, he loves; seven, she loves;
Eight, they both love.
Nine, he comes; ten, he tarries;
Eleven, he courts; twelve, he marries.

March winds and April showers
Bring forth May flowers.

The cock crows in the morn
To tell us to rise,
And he that lies late
Will never be wise;
For early to bed
And early to rise
Is the way to be healthy
And wealthy and wise.

Pat-a-cake, pat-a-cake, baker's man,
Bake me a cake as fast as you can;
Pat it and prick it and mark it with a B,
And put it in the oven for Baby and me.

The fair maid who, the first of May,
Goes to the fields at break of day,
And bathes in dew from the hawthorn tree
Will ever after handsome be.

June brings tulips, lilies, roses,
Fills the children's hands with posies.

Birds of a feather flock together,
So will pigs and swine;
Rats and mice will have their choice,
And so will I have mine.

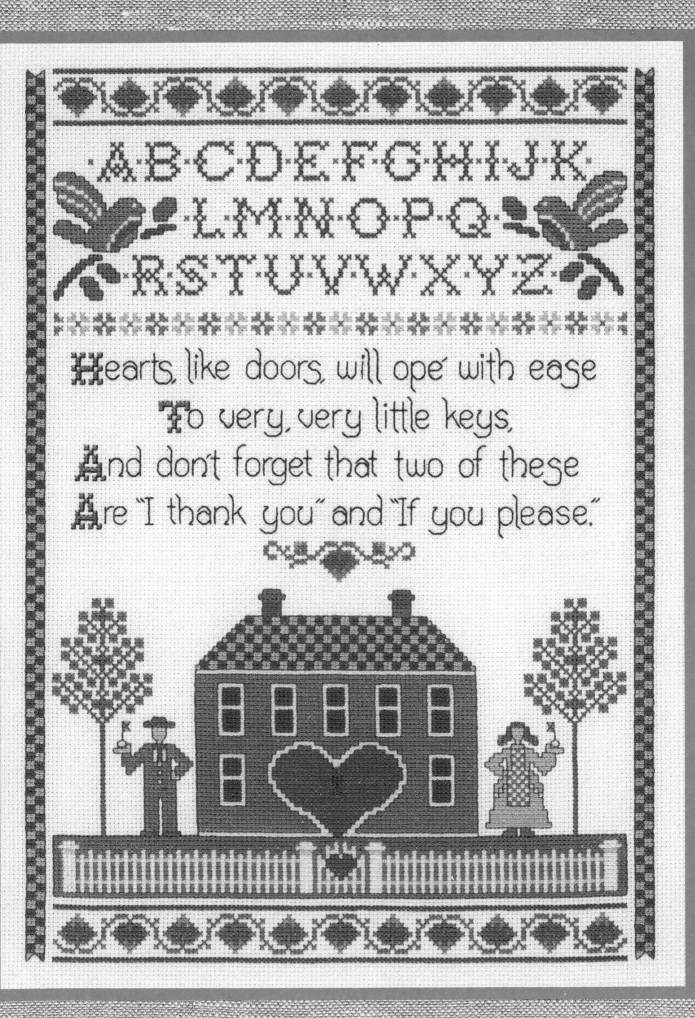

ABCDEFGHIJK
LMNOPQ
RSTUVWXYZ

Hearts, like doors, will ope' with ease
To very, very little keys,
And don't forget that two of these
Are "I thank you" and "If you please."

Good, better, best; never rest
Till Good be Better and Better, Best.

Jenny Wren last week was wed,
  And built her nest in Grandpa's shed;
Look next week and you shall see
  Two little eggs, and maybe three.

Winter's
Slippy, Drippy,
Nippy.

Spring is
Showery,
Flowery,
Bowery.

JULY

Hot July brings cooling showers,
Apricots, and gillyflowers.

Little drops of water,
Little grains of sand,
Make the mighty ocean
And the pleasant land.

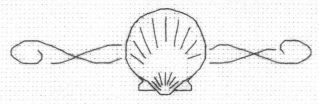

I like little pussy,
Her coat is so warm,
And if I don't hurt her,
She'll do me no harm.

So I'll not pull her tail,
Nor drive her away,
But pussy and I
Very gently will play.

Pussycat, pussycat, where have you been?
I've been to London to look at the queen.
Pussycat, pussycat, what did you there?
I frightened a little mouse under her chair.

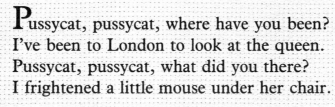

There was once a fish. (What more could you wish?)
He lived in the sea. (Where else would he be?)
He was caught on a line. (Whose line if not mine?)
So I brought him to you. (What else should I do?)

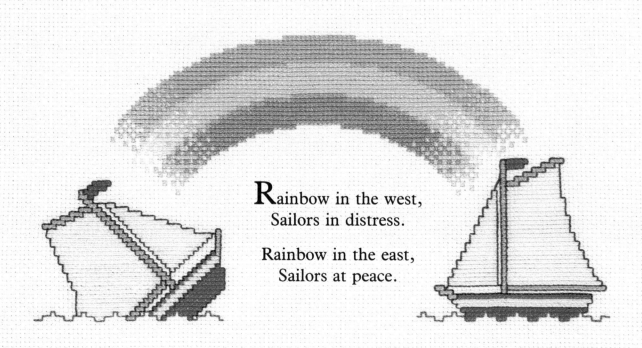

Rainbow in the west,
Sailors in distress.

Rainbow in the east,
Sailors at peace.

Jack and Jill went up the hill,
To fetch a pail of water;
Jack fell down and broke his crown,
And Jill came tumbling after.

August brings the sheaves of corn,
Then the harvest home is borne.

All work and no play makes Jack a dull boy,
All play and no work makes Jack a mere toy.

If you are to be a gentleman,
As I suppose you'll be,
You'll neither laugh nor smile,
For a tickling of the knee.

Calico pie, the little birds fly
Down to the calico tree.
Their wings were blue
And they sang "Tilly-loo"
Till away they all flew,
And they never came back to me.

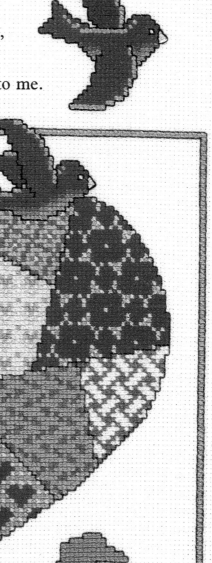

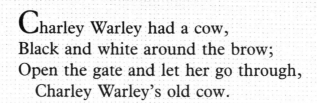

Charley Warley had a cow,
Black and white around the brow;
Open the gate and let her go through,
Charley Warley's old cow.

Sleep, baby, sleep,
Thy father guards the sheep,
Thy mother shakes the dreamland tree,
And from it fall sweet dreams for thee,
Sleep, baby, sleep.

SEPTEMBER

September offers breezes soft
Until the fruit is in the loft.

There's a neat little clock,
  In the schoolroom it stands,
And it points to the time
  With its two little hands.

And may we, like the clock,
  Keep a face clean and bright,
With hands ever ready
  To do what is right.

had a little

Its fleece was white as

And everywhere that went

The was sure to go.

It followed her to one day,

was against the

It made the laugh and play

To see a at

Monday's child is fair of face,
Tuesday's child is full of grace,
Wednesday's child is full of woe,
Thursday's child has far to go,
Friday's child is loving and giving,
Saturday's child works hard for his living,
And the child that is born on the Sabbath day
Is bonny and blithe, and good and gay.

I had a little hobby horse
And it was dapple gray,
Its head was made of pea-straw,
Its tail was made of hay.

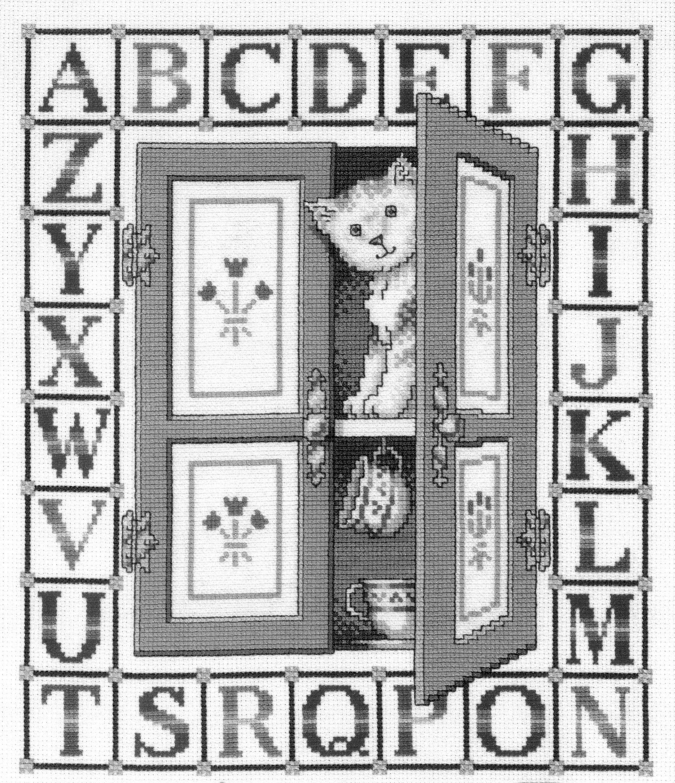

A B C D E F F G

Z   G
                            H
Y   I
                            J
X   K
                            L
W   M
V
U   T S R Q P O N

Great A, little a, bouncing B,
The cats in the cupboard
And can't see me.

Fresh October brings the pheasant;
Then to gather nuts is pleasant.

To make your candles last for a',
You wives and maids give ear-o!
To put them out's the only way,
Says honest John Bolde'ro.

Tommy's tears and Mary's fears
Will make them old before their years.

Three little ghostesses, sitting on postesses,
Eating buttered toastesses, greasing their fistesses,
Up to their wristesses, oh, what beastesses
To make such feastesses.

Catch him, crow! Carry him, kite!
Take him away till the apples are ripe;
When they are ripe and ready to fall,
Here comes baby, apples and all!

If you are not handsome at twenty,
Not strong at thirty,
Not rich at forty,
Not wise at fifty,
You never will be.

Good night, sleep tight,
Wake up bright in the morning light,
To do what's right with all your might.

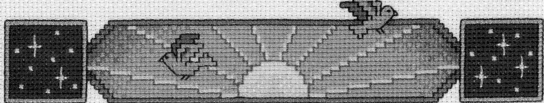

N·O·V·E·M·B·E·R

Dull November brings the blast;
Then the leaves are whirling fast.

A wise old owl sat in an oak.
The more he heard, the less he spoke;
The less he spoke, the more he heard.
Why aren't we all like that wise old bird?

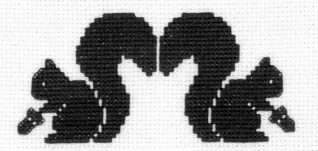

Wee Willie Winkie
Runs through the town,
Upstairs, downstairs,
In his nightgown,
Rapping at the window,
Crying through the lock,
Are the children in their beds,
For now it's eight o'clock?

The boughs do shake, the bells do ring,
So merrily comes our harvest in,
   Our harvest in, our harvest in,
So merrily comes our harvest in.
   We've ploughed, we've sowed,
   We've reaped, we've mowed,
   We've got our harvest in.

Ride away, ride away,
   Johnny shall ride,
He shall have a pussycat
   Tied to one side;
He shall have a little dog
   Tied to the other,
And Johnny shall ride
   To see his grandmother.

DECEMBER

Chill December brings the sleet,
Blazing fire, and Christmas treat.

Smiling girls, rosy boys,
  Come and buy my little toys,
Monkeys made of gingerbread,
  And sugar horses painted red.

Christmas is coming,
The geese are getting fat,
Please to put a penny
In an old man's hat.
If you haven't got a penny,
A ha'penny will do;
If you haven't got a ha'penny,
Then God bless you.

When December snows fall fast,
Marry, and true love will last.

Little Jack Horner sat in a corner,
  Eating of Christmas pie;
He put in his thumb and pulled out a plum,
  And said "What a good boy am I!"

Golden slumbers kiss your eyes,
Smiles awake you when you rise,
Sleep, pretty baby; do not cry,
And I will sing you a lullaby.

MOTHER GOOSE
AND THE SAMPLER

Mother Goose and the traditional sampler, two of our most beloved artifacts of bygone days, have much in common: Both employed rhymes to reveal their wisdom and both began their rise in popularity at about the same time. Additionally, each had long and colorful histories before finally settling comfortably into the laps of children, whose loving embrace of Mother Goose's nonsense and wisdom helped create for the verses a prominent niche in our literary heritage. And youthful hands helped transform the sampler from a schoolroom exercise into a unique and expressive art form.

Examplars

Mention samplers today and many people think only of cross-stitch. Long ago, however, samplers or "examplars," as they were once known, displayed a variety of stitches, designs, and color combinations. Before there were printed patterns, women shared and exchanged needlework ideas, quickly copying swatches of new work before they could be forgotten. A strip of linen was reserved as a "notebook" on which designs were placed haphazardly until the cloth was filled. These samplers were highly valued, and handed down through generations. As printed pattern books became common, the practical record-keeping sampler fell into disuse. Thereafter, only the children who still required practice, stitched designs and letters on samplers.

American Samplers

Samplers already had a long and rich tradition by the time the first settlers sailed for North America in the seventeenth century. While the early American colonists took great pride in their independence of religious thought, their style and artistic taste remained decidedly English. The earliest surviving American sampler was completed by Loara Standish around the year 1645 (Fig. 1), and is indistinguishable from English samplers of that time.

From the earliest days, Massachusetts towns emphasized reading—not for educational purposes, but so people could read their Bibles. Within a century of arrival—Massachusetts Bay Colony was first settled in 1630—schools began springing up. An early Boston school for girls advertised its priorities with ". . . a Boarding School, where will

be Carefully taught Flourishing, Embroidery and all sorts of Needlework, also Filigree, Painting on Glass, writing, arithmetick and singing Psalm Tunes."

Many girls (and a few boys) from four to fifteen years old worked a simple alphabet sampler at home or in a local dame school. Only well-to-do

"Loara Standish is my name/Lord guide my heart that I may do thy will/And fill my hands with such convenient skill/As will conduce to virtue devoid of shame/And I will give glory to thy name."

Loara Standish, daughter of the legendary Captain Miles Standish, is considered to be the first girl to complete a sampler on American soil. The work is stylistically consistent with English samplers, many of which were brought to North America with other household belongings. Typical of the craftsmanship of the day, the front and back are mirror images of one another.

Fig. 1
(Photograph courtesy of The Pilgrim Society, Plymouth, Massachusetts.)

girls went on to the costly private schools or academies. There they produced elaborate samplers, adding verses, pastoral scenes, flowers, and fanciful animals to their alphabets. The finished works represented the girls' maturity and accomplishments. They were usually signed, dated, framed, and proudly displayed on the walls of the family home.

Throughout the eighteenth century, regional differences began to appear. New patterns were developed, often unique to an area, city, or school. Some patterns remained isolated while others gained wide popularity. Adam and Eve with the serpent, seen on Mary Emmon's sampler (Fig. 2), appeared in Boston and spread quickly to other areas. The Balch School of Providence, Rhode Island, often

"Mary Emmons Wrought this Sampler/in the Thirteen year of hir Age August 8 1749/Behold Alass Our Days We Spend/How vain they be how soon they End"

Mary Emmons's sampler is one of a distinctive group of samplers featuring the "Boston band pattern," just below the top alphabet. This band was peculiar to the Boston area and remained popular until the 1820's. Adam and Eve were also common on needlework from this area, sometimes charmingly attired in proper colonial dress.

Fig. 2

(Photograph from *American Needlework Treasures: Samplers and Silk Embroideries from the Collection of Betty Ring.* Copyright © 1987 by Betty Ring, E. P. Dutton.)

featured two trumpeting angels and an imposing floral border. The schools around Portland, Maine, usually featured verse and genealogy, along with local scenes, all surrounded by rose and vine borders. On the whole, samplers of this period displayed many distinctive styles, establishing them as uniquely American.

By the beginning of the nineteenth century, the popularity of samplers was at its peak. A school's reputation could rest almost entirely on the style, quality, and originality of the samplers its students produced. These were complex pieces, heavily influenced by the school mistresses who probably drew their own designs, thereby accounting for the similarity of samplers from any particular school. Increased emphasis on academics gave rise to map samplers and cross-stitched multiplication tables. Large depictions of the school itself, painstakingly stitched brick by brick, were not uncommon. Memorial embroideries, an outgrowth of the sampler, usually featuring a lady bent weeping by a monument beneath a willow tree, became tremendously popular after the death of George Washington. Yet even within the strictest guidelines, young girls often managed to create very personal, very expressive works of art. They portrayed their homes, families, pets, and gardens. Their youthful fantasies were embodied in florid scenes of courting couples. Occasionally the true child would shine

through the most formal exercise, as did one little girl who stitched across the bottom of her Washington Memorial sampler, "Patty Polk did this and she hated every stitch she did in it. She loves to read much more."

Serious sampler work waned by the mid-nineteenth century as the country moved toward public schooling. But many decades later these classroom exercises caught the eye of collectors. For the American-schoolgirl sampler was unique. Betty Ring, the noted sampler historian and collector, writes:

> *The tolerance of child-like imperfections, particularly in lettering, made American samplers conspicuously different from English ones. The strict English schoolmistress would rarely accept such mistakes, and a girl was forced to correct her work until she arrived at perfection. Yet today, informality in design and traces of childish impatience lend charm to American samplers and convey a sense of youthful innocence more appealing than flawless execution.*

Reality, it seems, was seldom a requirement in samplers. People were often bigger than houses, dogs might be indistinguishable from cats (and cats indistinguishable from lions), and letters sometimes landed in improbable places. Rarely has any other art form captured so well the innocence and spirit of childhood.

Sampler Verses and Mother Goose

Elaborate samplers nearly always included verses, usually stressing virtue, goodness, and industry. Isaac Watts's *Divine Songs for Children* appears to have been a popular source for many needleworkers, but the Bible, Shakespeare, and other authors are represented as well. The most commonly occurring verse is religious:

> *Jesus permit thy gracious name to stand*
> *As the first efforts of an infant's hand*
> *And while her fingers o're this canvas move*
> *Engage her tender heart to seek thy love*
> *May she with thy dear children share a part*
> *And write thy name thyself upon her heart.*

The mature, often morbid themes of many verses seem incongruous with the delicate age of the child wielding needle and thread, as in this verse from a nine-year-old:

> *Cordelia L Bennet is My Name*
> *New york is My Station*
> *Heaven is my Dwelling Place*
> *and Christ is My Salvation*
> *When I am Dead and in my Grave*
> *and all my Bones are Rotten*
> *When This you See Remember me*
> *That I Be not Forgotten*

Occasionally the carefree child is glimpsed through the words, but even then the stern gaze of the mistress can be felt:

> The trees were green/The sun was hot
> Sometimes I worked/And sometimes not
> Seven years my age/My name Jane Grey,
> And often much/Too fond of play.

Here is one from the "all hands must be busy" school of thought:

> This needle work of Mine doth tell
> When a child is learned well
> By my parents I was taught
> Not to spend my time for naught.

Throughout the eighteenth century, sampler work by children kept pace with the growing popularity of printed nursery rhyme books. Yet, surprisingly, these rhymes were rarely stitched by the children who loved them. Apparently such frivolous verses were considered unfit to appear on a needlework that was meant to show the maturity and discipline of its maker. Nevertheless many of the verses in these early books and verses on the samplers appear to have had common sources. The Fleetwood–Quincy sampler (1654) displays this inscription:

> In prosperity friends are plenty
> In adversity not one in twenty.

Later Mother Goose tells us:

> In time of prosperity, friends will be plenty
> In time of adversity, not one in twenty.

An eighteenth century sampler declares:

> Labor for learning before you grow old
> For it is better than silver or gold
> When silver is gone and money is spent
> Then learning is most excellent.

Mother Goose recites a shorter version:

> When land is gone and money spent
> Then learning is most excellent.

In another parallel a sampler notes:

> Could we with ink the Ocean fill
> Were the whole earth of parchment made
> Were every single stick a Quill
> And every man a scribe by trade
> To write the love of God above
> Would drain the Ocean dry.

Says Mother Goose in an obvious parody:

> If all the world were paper,
> And all the sea were ink;
> If all the trees were bread and cheese,
> What should we have to drink?

There are other examples of verses appearing both on samplers and in Mother Goose volumes, but all of them fall into the category of proverbs or old sayings drawn from the great pool of our cultural heritage. These words of wisdom give us insight into how people lived and learned in earlier centuries. They distill hard-earned knowledge and beliefs into tiny bright gems that a child can hold and cherish and pass along to the next child.

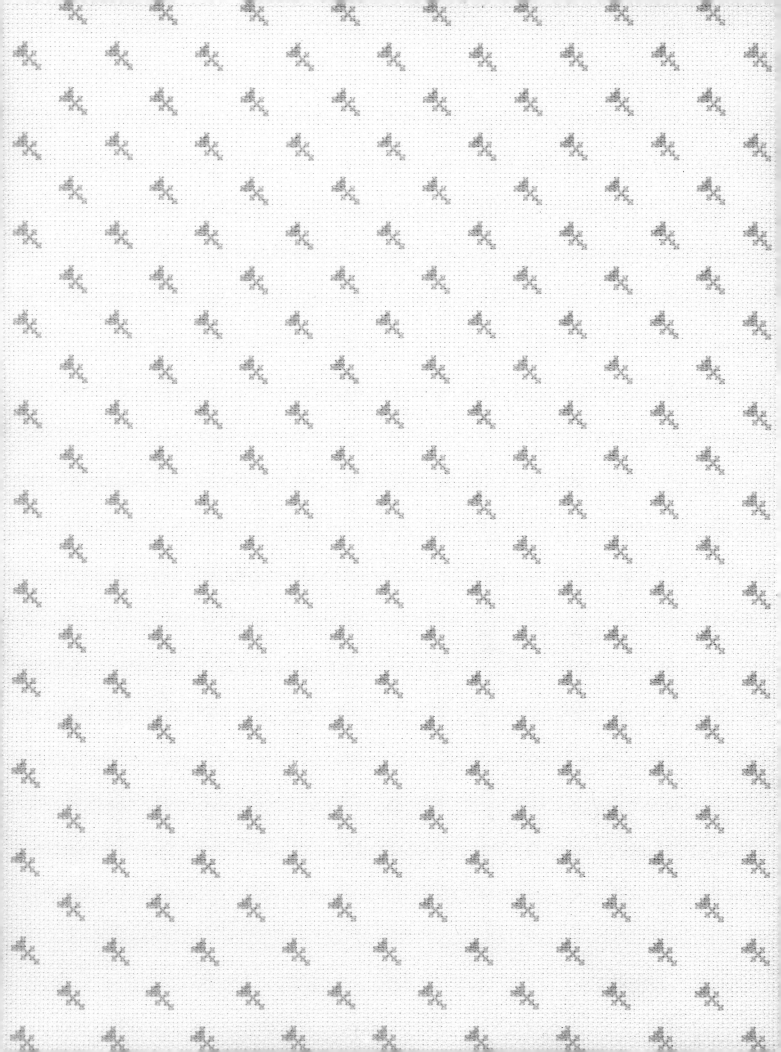

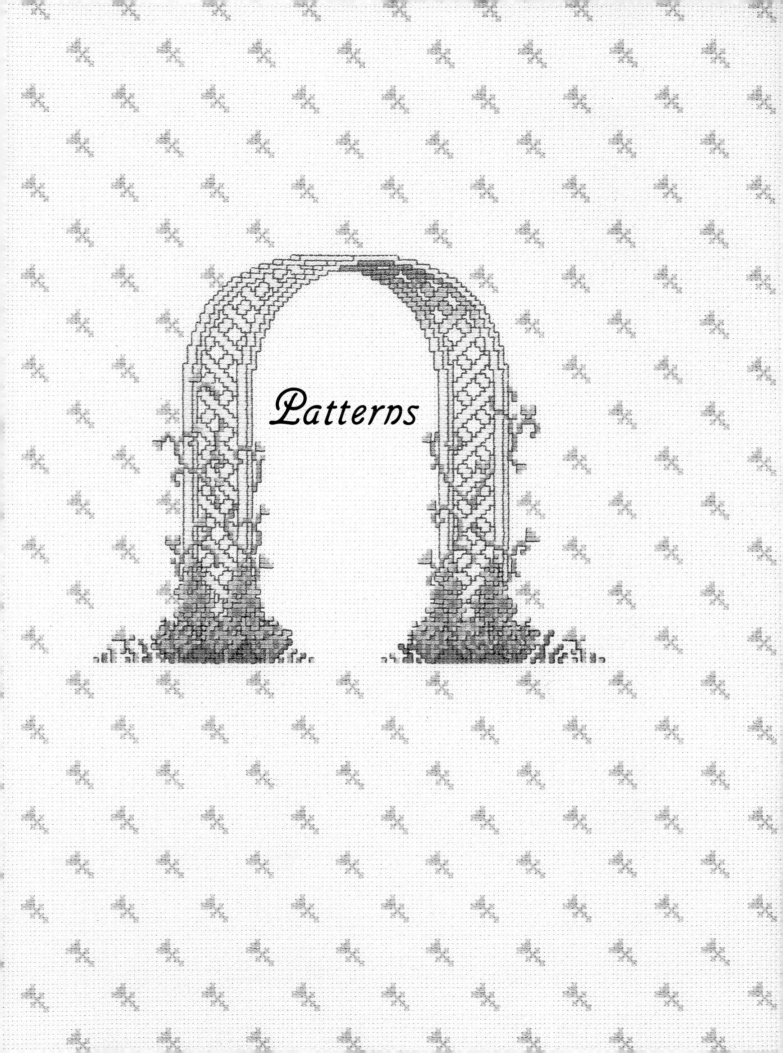

Patterns

CROSS-STITCH ESSENTIALS

Needles and ribbons and packets of pins
Prints and chintz and odd bod-a-kins;
They'd never mind whether
You laid them together
Or one from the other in packets and tins.

Cross-stitch is quick and easy to master, applicable to dozens of decorative projects, and adjustable to busy schedules —is it any wonder that counting stitches currently reigns as the queen of the needlework arts? With a vocabulary of only a few simple stitches, a wide range of designs is available to both the novice and the experienced needleworker. The basic instructions will help you recreate these family heirlooms.

Materials

FABRICS

Cross-stitch requires even-weave fabric, which means the length-wise (warp) threads are the same thickness as the cross-wise (woof) threads. This even grid of threads allows the cross-stitch X to form a perfect square. Fabrics especially developed for cross-stitch are available in most needlework shops. Before purchasing, always make sure your fabric is colorfast.

Aida Cloth—Ideal for both beginners and advanced stitchers, this 100% cotton fabric has a surface of clearly designated squares. All aida fabric has a *count*, which refers to the number of squares to one inch and thus, the number of stitches per inch. The higher the count, the smaller the finished stitchery will be. Aida ranges from 6-count to 18-count and is available in a wide range of colors. Most of the projects in this book were worked on 14-count aida. However, measurements for other aida counts are given with each pattern so you may choose the finished size that best suits your purposes.

Hardanger—This is another name for 22-count aida cloth. Actually, each count of aida once had a specific name, but hardanger is the only one still in common use.

Linen—A popular traditional fabric for cross-stitch, linen is available in a wide range of thread counts and colors. The thread thickness is slightly less even and the weave is finer, so working on linen makes it a bit more difficult to count the spaces. However, nothing surpasses this fabric in beauty and longevity. Finer weaves, such as 32-count linen, are usually stitched "over two," meaning the cross-stitch spans two threads both vertically and horizontally.

Waste Canvas—This special even-weave fabric allows cross-stitch to be worked on other kinds of fabric, or on purchased items such as aprons and sweatshirts. The weave of the project must be fairly tight. To work with waste canvas, first align the weave of the waste canvas to the weave of the fabric and baste the waste canvas in the area you wish to stitch. Second, using the waste canvas as a guide for stitch placement, work the cross-stitch through the smallest holes and penetrate both thicknesses. Third, when all cross-stitch is completed, moisten the canvas. Then carefully pull out all horizontal threads of the waste canvas, one at a time. Working in the same manner, remove all vertical threads. Finally, rinse the project thoroughly to remove any waste canvas starch.

THREADS

A vast array of rich colors and thread fibers is readily available for cross-stitch embroidery. Always check to see that the thread you are purchasing is colorfast.

Six-Strand Embroidery Floss—This is the most common thread used for cross-stitch. It is 100% cotton and available in hundreds of shades. Floss, as it is usually called, easily separates into six strands; the number of strands you use depends on the count of your fabric.

Silk Floss—Luxurious silk, available in a wide range of colors, can be used in cross-stitch, but requires a fairly experienced needleworker. The fiber snags and wears thin more quickly than cotton. However, for excellent color and longevity, silk cannot be equaled.

Tools

NEEDLES

Blunt points and long, narrow eyes make tapestry needles ideal for cross-stitch. The blunt point prevents splitting fibers and threads, and the large eye accommodates multiple strands of embroidery floss. Tapestry needles range in size from 13 (heavy) to 26 (fine). No. 24, with 2 or 3 strands floss, works well with cross-stitch for 11- or 14-count aida. For backstitch, use a slightly finer needle to prevent fabric holes from becoming clogged.

HOOPS

Whether an embroidery hoop is required depends on the fabric. Some cross-stitch fabric (such as aida) is heavily sized, making the cloth stiff enough so that when one is stitching, the squares retain their shape. Softer fabrics, however, do require a hoop. Various diameter hoops accommodate many project sizes. The size of the hoop depends on the size of the fabric; there should be enough fabric so that the drum of the hoop is tight all around. Check wooden hoops to see that they are free of splinters that can snag fabric and thread. If splinters are present, pad the hoop by wrapping it in thin, white muslin. Plastic hoops also work well.

FRAMES

Needlework frames are used in the same fashion as hoops and are available in a large selection of designs. Large oval or circular hoops mounted to a free-standing frame are convenient since the fabric never has to be removed once work is started. Rectangular scroll frames hold the fabric at top and bottom, and you can roll to a desired section of the design. While needlework frames are not very portable, they do save the fabric from excessive handling.

SCISSORS

Keep two pairs of scissors in your needlework basket: a large pair for cutting fabric and a small pair of very sharp, pointed embroidery scissors for cutting thread. If an area of stitching needs to be removed, the small scissors should be able to slip under the tiny cross-stitches to snip them one at a time.

A FEW EXTRAS

Thread Organizer—There are several styles of thread organizers available; they protect the floss and make colors easier to organize.

Graph Paper—When personalizing a design with names or other text, graph paper is needed to chart and position the letters.

Washable Marker—For any small marks you might want to make on the fabric, use a washable marker, tested for needlework.

Tweezers—For any area of stitching you need to remove, snip the thread with embroidery scissors, then pull the thread pieces out with tweezers.

Getting Ready

CUTTING ENOUGH FABRIC

Always allow ample margins around the design area. To provide enough excess cloth, fabric measurements generally should include at least a three-inch margin all around. (Three-inch margins have been allowed for in the fabric measurements in this book.)

FINISHING THE EDGES

To prevent the fabric edges from fraying, they must be fixed before beginning the cross-stitch. A sewing machine zig-zag stitch holds well, as do commercial liquid binders designed for that purpose. If you prefer hemming the edges, allow extra fabric in addition to the three-inch margin. Masking tape is sometimes suggested to bind edges, but it can be hazardous because the adhesive remains on the fabric when the tape is removed.

FINDING THE CENTER

Fold the fabric in half, both lengthwise and widthwise; lightly crease the folds. With a contrasting color sewing thread, sew basting lines along the creases. The intersection of the basting lines is the exact center of the fabric, and the lines mark the cloth into quarters. For a very small piece of cross-stitch, you might want to mark the center with a washable marker, thereby eliminating the need for the basting lines.

READING A CHART

Each square on the chart grid corresponds to one count on the fabric, be it working over one square on aida cloth, or two or more threads of linen. Each symbol on the grid represents one cross-stitch in a specific color; the color key with the chart designates the color. Find the center of the chart by following the arrows at the side edges; the intersection of the chart arrows corresponds with the intersection of basting stitches on the fabric. Begin working the chart at the center. If you plan to personalize the chart with a name or initials, draw them in place before beginning the cross-stitch.

HOW MANY STRANDS?

The number of strands of embroidery floss you use depends on the count of your fabric. Cross-stitch on 14- to 18-count fabric

uses 2 or 3 strands floss, depending on how saturated you want the color. On the same count fabric, backstitch with 1 or 2 strands, for you should work this outline stitch with one strand less than cross-stitch. Before starting your cross-stitch, experiment with scrap fabric and floss to achieve the texture and color level you want. And remember that while having more strands allows for heavier color, it will also make the finished project considerably bulkier. For a framed picture, this makes little difference, but for a bib or towel trim, flexibility might be more desirable.

DMC Six-Strand Embroidery Floss was used to execute all designs in *Mother Goose's Words of Wit and Wisdom*, and all color numbers and number of strands used refer to that thread.

Stitching

STARTING THE THREAD

Work with 12″ to 18″ lengths of floss. Separate all six strands (called *stranding*), then recombine the number of threads required. Stranded thread allows for better coverage. To begin stitching, bring the needle up through the fabric and leave about 1″ thread on the back side. Plan to work your first four or five cross-stitches over the thread end on the back side of the fabric.

THE CROSS-STITCH

The completed cross-stitch forms a square X. Two stitches make up that X and great care must be taken that all the top stitches are positioned in the same direction. (Arrows indicate the direction of cross-stitches.)

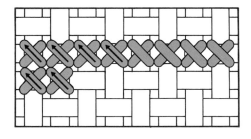

To Work a Single Cross-stitch
Bring the needle up at the corner (A), and down through the opposite diagonal corner (B). To complete the second half of the stitch, bring the needle up at the lower remaining corner of the square (C), and down through the last corner of the same square (D).

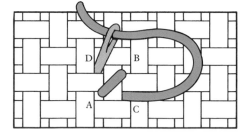

To Work a Row of Cross-stitch
Work from left to right making the lower diagonal half of each cross-stitch; then return, right to left, making the upper diagonal half of each stitch. Take care to keep the stitch tension uniform throughout; stitches that are too tight will distort the fabric and stitches that are too loose will distort the design and create an uneven surface texture.

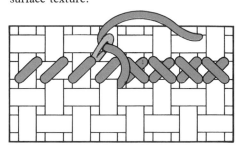

To Work a Quarter-Cross
When a color symbol occupies only half of a chart square and is bound by a diagonal backstitching line (see below, far left), bring the needle up at corner (A) and down through the center of the square (B). Later, the backstitch will finish the stitch.

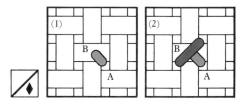

(1) Quarter-cross stitch (2) Backstitch over quarter-cross stitch

A chart square with two color symbols, separated by a diagonal backstitch, requires two quarter stitches. Backstitch will later finish the square.

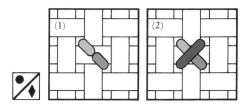

(1) Two quarter-cross stitches (2) Backstitch over quarter stitches

To Work a Three-Quarter Cross
When a color symbol occupies only half of the square, and is not bounded by a line of backstitch but by a fine diagonal line, bring the needle up at (A), down at (B), up through the corner of the square at (C), and down at (D). As always, be sure the upper half of the stitch is in the same direction as the other cross-stitches. (Arrows

indicate direction of cross-stitches.) When two color symbols occupy one chart square, but are separated by a fine diagonal line, one color will be a three-quarter cross-stitch, the other color a quarter-cross. The stronger color is the three-quarter cross.

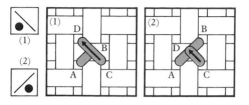

To Work a Two-Square Diagonal
When this configuration (below, far left) appears on a chart, use a three-quarter cross-stitch in square (A), nothing in square (B). Later, the backstitch diagonally runs the full length of the two squares.

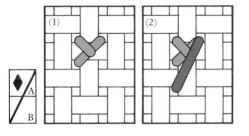

(1) Three-quarter stitch appearing in square A
(2) Backstitch over three-quarter stitch

BACKSTITCH
Used for outline, backstitch adds emphasis to a cross-stitch area. Bring the needle up at (A), down at (B), up at (C), down at (A), up at (D), down at (C), and so forth. As always, keep the tension of the stitches even.

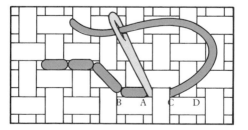

FRENCH KNOT
Ideal for eyes or doorknobs, the French knot adds just a dot of color. Bring the needle up through the fabric at (A) and hold the floss with your other hand. Wrap the floss around the needle once. Keep holding the floss and insert the needle beside (A), catching at least one thread of

the fabric. With the other hand helping to guide the floss, pull the needle through from below to tighten the knot. The size

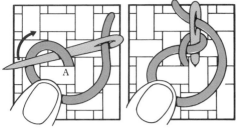

of the knot depends on how many strands you use. For example, one strand will provide a very fine knot, two strands will be heavier, and so on. In most cases, 2 strands on 14-count aida works well.

BLENDED NEEDLE
A cross-stitch using 2 or more strands floss, each strand in a different color.

FINISHING THE THREAD
When a length of thread has been used up, secure the end by running the needle under about five stitches on the back side of the fabric. Clip any excess close to the fabric.

CARRYING THE THREAD
When moving the same color from one stitched area to another, do not carry the floss for more than one-half inch at the back of the work. If thread must be carried a longer distance, cut the floss and start over again in the new section. Keep in mind that dark threads will show through light fabrics and light threads will show through dark. Whenever possible, run floss behind areas that are already filled with cross-stitch.

Finishing

CHECKING IT OVER
When you have finished the design, put it away for a couple of days. Then make a methodical inspection of your stitchery and compare it to the pattern to check for any overlooked stitches.

CLEANING
Wash gently and briefly in cool water with mild soap flakes. Do not rub the stitchery surface. Rinse thoroughly in cool water, but do not wring out. Roll the project in a dry towel to absorb the water. Unroll, right side down, on a clean, dry towel. Cover with a light-weight fabric (such as a sheet) and press with the iron on "cotton" setting until the needlework is dry. Do not dry clean.

BLOCKING
A frame shop experienced in handling needlework is one option. If you prefer to frame your own work, a cork bulletin board with wooden frame is perfect for blocking. Cover the cork with a piece of

clean, pressed muslin. Place the needlework, right side up, on the muslin and dampen well with a mist bottle. Align the fabric grain to the straight edge of the bulletin board and, keeping the fabric taut, anchor the corners with push pins. Next, pin the midpoints at each side, then add pins about every half-inch all around. Allow the fabric to dry completely.

MOUNTING
Using acid-free mat board (available from art supply stores), cut two pieces at least three-quarters of an inch larger all around than the desired finished size. Tape the boards together on all edges. Cut a piece of polyester quilt batting the same size as the boards. Wrap a sheet of clean, pressed, white muslin over the batting; tape excess fabric at back of board. Center the needlework, right side up, on the covered board. Keeping the needlework taut, push straight pins through the fabric and into the edges of the board. Secure the side edges with archival tape. Using acid-free materials, frame the mounted needlework as desired. A note of caution: Do not allow glass to press against the stitchery surface.

Helps, Hints, Tips

- Do not pre-wash aida cloth.

- If you use an embroidery hoop, center and secure the fabric in place. When finished for the day, remove the work from the hoop, for the pressure crushes the stitches between the rings and that results in an uneven surface texture. Hoop marks also occur when skin oils and soil build up on the fabric around the hoop edge. Repositioning the hoop often will prevent this.

- Take great care to keep your work clean. Always wash your hands before starting your embroidery. When the unfinished project is set aside for the day, roll in tissue.

- When finished with your cross-stitch for the day, park your sewing needle at the outer edges of the fabric. If a rust stain develops, it will not show in the margins.

- Pricked fingers, the battle scars of needleworkers, sometimes result in blood staining the fabric. If this happens, immediately wash the cloth in cold water using mild soap flakes.

- If you need to store your cross-stitch for a lengthy period, roll the piece in acid-free tissue, then store the roll in a clean pillow case. Needlework should not be stored in plastic bags, for the fabric needs to breathe.

- Framed needlework pictures should not hang on the outer house walls, for moisture may intrude through the back. Also avoid showing off your masterpiece on a wall receiving direct sunlight, for that will cause fading.

GARDEN ARCH

Shown on page 1

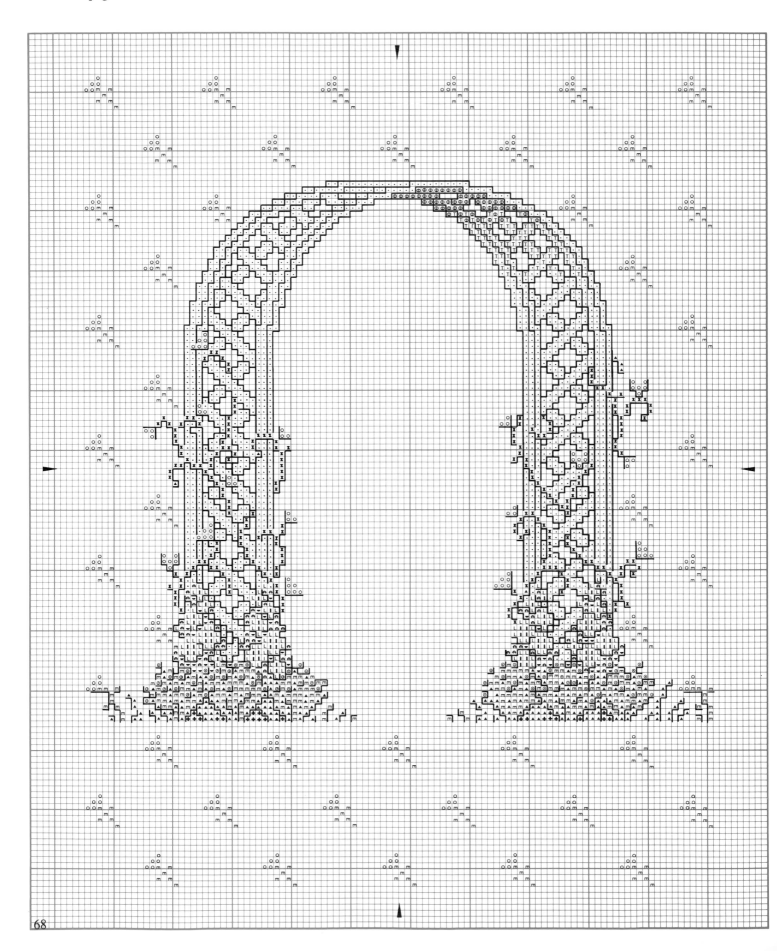

MY MELODIES

Shown on page 7

The garden arch serves equally well as a birth, wedding, or anniversary commemorative. See alphabets 1 and 2 on page 156 to chart the names, dates, or whatever is required. Center each line of lettering within the arch and position the lavender flowers as needed to fill space or to separate lines.

The original design was worked on aida 14 using 3 strands embroidery floss for cross-stitch and 2 strands for backstitch. Before starting, see *How Many Strands*, page 66.

Fabric	Design size	Fabric size for project shown
Aida 11	9½″ × 12¼″	16″ × 19″
Aida 14	7¾″ × 9¾″	14″ × 16″
Aida 18	5⅞″ × 7½″	12″ × 14″
Hardanger 22	4¾″ × 6⅛″	10″ × 12″
Linen 32 (over 2)	6½″ × 8½″	12″ × 14″

DMC Six-Strand Floss

Cross-stitch

· ·		white
o o	211	lavender, lt.
⊙ ⊙	318	steel grey, lt.
+ +	502	blue-green
▾ ▾	563	jade, lt.
o o	744	yellow, pale
T T	762	pearl grey, v. lt.
L L	776	pink, med.
I I	894	carnation, v. lt.
∩ ∩	955	nile green, lt.
m m	964	seagreen, lt.
▲ ▲	992	aquamarine
× ×	993	aquamarine, lt.

Backstitch

	208	*lettering*
	501	*vines, plants*
	840	*archway*

French knot

•	208	*punctuation*

The original design was worked on aida 14 using 3 strands embroidery floss for cross-stitch and 2 strands for backstitch. Before starting, see *How Many Strands*, page 66.

Fabric	Design size	Fabric size for project shown
Aida 11	8¼″ × 10½″	14″ × 16½″
Aida 14	6½″ × 8¼″	12½″ × 14″
Aida 18	5″ × 6⅜″	11″ × 12½″
Hardanger 22	4¼″ × 5¼″	10″ × 11″
Linen 32 (over 2)	5⅝″ × 7¼″	11½″ × 13″

Cross-stitch

· ·		white
L L	210	lavender, med.
o o	353	peach flesh
∴ ∴	776	pink, med.
▲ ▲	930	antique blue, dk.
× ×	3609	plum, ultra lt.

Backstitch

	930	*music notes, lettering*

French knot

•	930	*punctuation*

THE NORTH WIND DOTH BLOW

Shown on page 8

The direction of the wind has always foretold much about the weather and other concerns of life. One proverb states, "When the wind is in the north, the skillful fisher goes not forth." Another claims with assurance that "a bleak wind, a biting frost, and a scolding wife come out of the north."

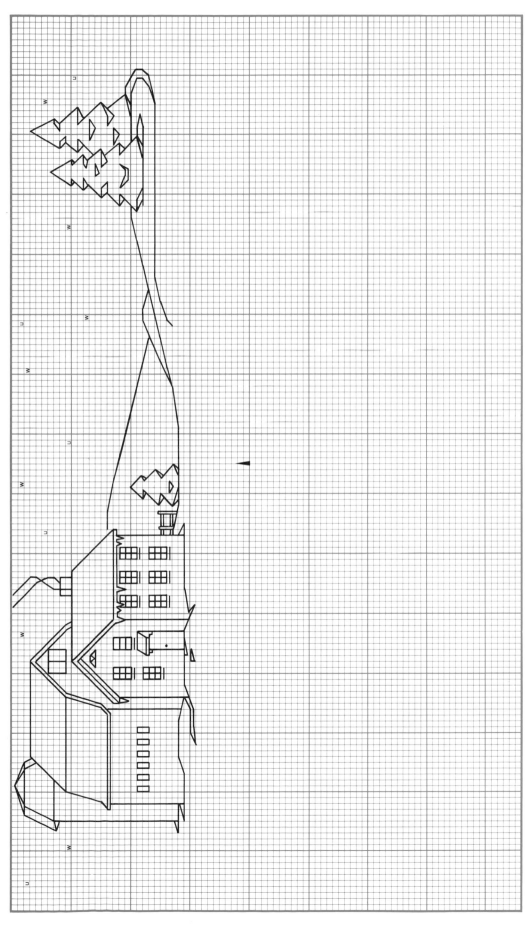

In the farm scene below the robin, the line does not always follow the grid from corner to corner. It was designed to resemble a freestyle line drawing. Follow the chart carefully.

Looking for a smaller project? Simply eliminate the snow and farm scene surrounding the robin.

The bird design was worked on aida 14 using 3 strands embroidery floss for cross-stitch and 2 strands for backstitch. The farm scene was worked with 1 strand. Before starting, see *How Many Strands*, page 66.

Fabric	Design size	Fabric size for project shown
Aida 11	13¾″ × 13¾″	20″ × 20″
Aida 14	10¾″ × 10¾″	17″ × 17″
Aida 18	8⅜″ × 8⅜″	14½″ × 14½″
Hardanger 22	6⅞″ × 6⅞″	13″ × 13″
Linen 32 (over 2)	9⅜″ × 9⅜″	15½″ × 15½″

DMC Six-Strand Floss

Cross-stitch

⌄ ⌄	221	shell pink, dk.
m m	223	shell pink, med.
T T	224	shell pink, lt.
× ×	311	navy blue, med.
W W	322	navy blue, v. lt.
■ ■	352	coral, lt.
ʊ ʊ	353	peach flesh
▲ ▲	355	terra cotta, dk.
Φ Φ	356	terra cotta, med.
I I	437	tan, lt.
ı ı	543	beige-brown, ultra lt.
+ +	632	rose brown, v. dk.
o o	676	old gold, lt.
· ·	712	cream
● ●	744	yellow, pale
L L	745	yellow, lt. pale
\ \	746	off white
† †	754	peach flesh, lt.
ʊ ʊ	760	salmon
o o	761	salmon, lt.
u u	794	cornflower blue, lt.
● ●	839	beige-brown, dk.
– –	840	beige-brown, med.
z z	841	beige-brown, lt.
n n	842	beige-brown, v. lt.
– –	948	peach flesh, v. lt.
ʌ ʌ	3064	rose brown, med.
✕ ✕	3328	salmon, med.

Backstitch

	311	*farm scene, smoke, outer frame*
	839	*bird, nest, barn wood*

French knot

•	311	*doorknob*
•	775	*bird's eye*

WHETHER IT'S COLD

Shown on page 9

Long ago, the weather on January 25th, St. Paul's Day, was always anxiously observed. Snow or rain foretold a dearth of grain; cloudy skies meant famine for bird or beast; strong winds were an omen of war. Clear and fair weather, to everyone's relief, forecast a happy year.

If snow does not suit your region of the country, feel free to change the snowflakes to raindrops (use DMC Six-Strand Embroidery Floss #800, pale delft).

The original design was worked on aida 14 using 3 strands embroidery floss for cross-stitch and 2 strands for backstitch. Before starting, see *How Many Strands*, page 66.

Fabric	Design size	Fabric size for project shown
Aida 11	11¾" × 15"	18" × 21"
Aida 14	9¼" × 11¾"	15" × 18"
Aida 18	7¼" × 9¼"	13" × 15"
Hardanger 22	5⅞" × 7½"	12" × 13½"
Linen 32 (over 2)	8⅛" × 10¼"	14" × 16"

DMC Six-Strand Floss

Cross-stitch

		white
	223	shell pink, med.
	224	shell pink, lt.
	225	shell pink, v. lt.
	312	navy blue, lt.
	320	pistachio green, med.
	322	navy blue, v. lt.
	334	baby blue, med.
	335	rose
	352	coral, lt.
	353	peach flesh
	356	terra cotta, med.
	415	pearl grey
	436	tan
	437	tan, lt.
	543	beige-brown, ultra lt.
	632	rose brown, v. dk.
	676	old gold, lt.
	712	cream
	738	tan, v. lt.
	739	tan, ultra lt.
	744	yellow, pale
	745	yellow, lt. pale
	754	peach flesh, lt.
	758	terra cotta, lt.
	762	pearl grey, v. lt.
	794	cornflower blue, lt.
	800	delft, pale
	841	beige-brown, lt.
	842	beige-brown, v. lt.
	899	rose, med.
	930	antique blue, dk.
	931	antique blue, med.
	932	antique blue, lt.
	948	peach flesh, v. lt.
	966	baby green, med.
	3064	rose brown, med.
	3326	rose, lt.
	3328	salmon, med.

Backstitch

| | 838 | *all* |

French knot

| | 838 | *punctuation* |

HOW MANY DAYS

Shown on page 11

Publishers have always recognized the commercial value in ascribing great educational benefits to even the simplest rhymes. The 1771 edition of Tom Thumb's Playbook *is subtitled* ". . . To allure Little Ones in the first Principles of Learning." *The days of the week are remembered in* "How Many Days," *which first appeared in print in 1805.*

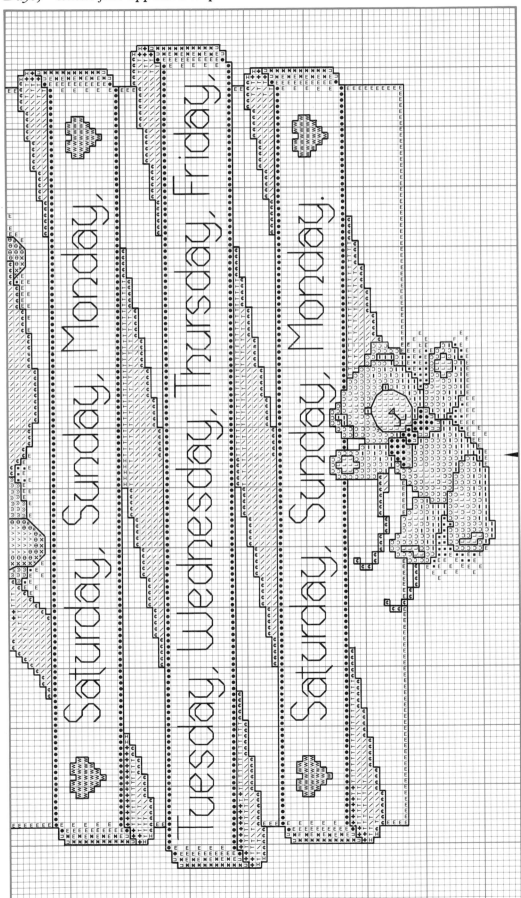

This little verse will brighten any infant's nursery and years later it will be a cherished reminder of the times when there was a toddler in the house. Stitch your child's initials into the toy blocks using alphabet 5 on page 156.

The original design was worked on aida 14 using 3 strands embroidery floss for cross-stitch and 2 strands for backstitch. Before starting, see *How Many Strands,* page 66.

Fabric	Design size	Fabric size for project shown
Aida 11	12¼″ × 18⅜″	18″ × 24½″
Aida 14	9¾″ × 14¾″	16″ × 21″
Aida 18	7½″ × 11⅜″	13½″ × 17½″
Hardanger 22	6¼″ × 9⅜″	12″ × 15½″
Linen 32 (over 2)	8½″ × 12¾″	14½″ × 19″

DMC Six-Strand Floss

Cross-stitch

∙∙		white
z z	211	lavender, lt.
∧ ∧	223	shell pink, med.
⫶ ⫶	318	steel grey, lt.
+ +	322	navy blue, v. lt.
T T	334	baby blue, med.
w w	353	peach flesh
– –	407	rose brown, dk.
n n	543	beige-brown, ultra lt.
∪ ∪	676	old gold, lt.
∴∴	712	cream
∾ ∾	744	yellow, pale
ı ı	746	off white
⊕ ⊕	754	peach flesh, lt.
x x	758	terra cotta, lt.
m m	762	pearl grey, v. lt.
I I	792	cornflower blue, dk.
∩ ∩	793	cornflower blue, med.
▶ ▶	839	beige-brown, dk.
∎ ∎	932	antique blue, lt.
v v	948	peach flesh, v. lt.
∘ ∘	950	rose brown, lt.
L L	951	rose brown, v. lt.
▾ ▾	955	nile green, lt.
● ●	962	dusty rose, med.
∘ ∘	3078	golden yellow, v. lt.
\ \	3325	baby blue
u u	3687	mauve

Backstitch

	839	*all art, lettering*

French knot

	839	*punctuation*

LAVENDER BLUE

Shown on page 12

HOW MANY DAYS

TEDDY BEAR ❧ Shown on page 11

When embroidering hands and faces, in order to create greater realism and expression, the backstitch line does not always run from corner to corner in the grid. Follow the chart carefully.

The original design was worked on aida 14 using 3 strands embroidery floss for cross-stitch and 2 strands for backstitch. Before starting, see *How Many Strands,* page 66.

Fabric	Design size	Fabric size for project shown
Aida 11	11″ × 11½″	17″ × 18″
Aida 14	8⅝″ × 9″	15″ × 15″
Aida 18	6⅝″ × 7″	13″ × 13″
Hardanger 22	5½″ × 5¾″	12″ × 12″
Linen 32 (over 2)	7½″ × 7⅞″	14″ × 14″

DMC Six-Strand Floss

Cross-stitch

∙∙		white
ı ı	211	lavender, lt.
●●	309	rose, deep
▲▲	335	rose
✕✕	340	blue violet, med.
◦◦	353	peach flesh
◡◡	407	rose brown, dk.
⊜⊜	436	tan
✱✱	437	tan, lt.
∩∩	554	violet, lt.
▪▪	632	rose brown, v. dk.
▪▪	676	old gold, lt.
ı ı	712	cream
⊃⊃	738	tan, v. lt.
╱╱	739	tan, ultra lt.
⊕⊕	744	yellow, pale
↑↑	746	off white
z z	754	peach flesh, lt.
u u	775	baby blue, lt.
I I	776	pink, med.
w w	793	cornflower blue, med.
∩∩	794	cornflower blue, lt.
⊙⊙	799	delft, med.
❤❤	800	delft, pale
⊤⊤	818	baby pink
╲╲	819	baby pink, lt.
m m	899	rose, med.
– –	948	peach flesh, v. lt.
∧∧	950	rose brown, lt.
∵∵	951	rose brown, v. lt.
✦✦	992	aquamarine
v v	993	aquamarine, lt.
s s	3078	golden yellow, v. lt.
○○	3326	rose, lt.

Cross-stitch, blended needle

✗✗	224/356	*(one strand each)*
ı ı	225/758	*(one strand each)*
L L	225/948	*(one strand each)*

Backstitch

	816	*background hearts*
	838	*children, large flowers, lettering*
	992	*flowers in boy's hand*

French knot

∙	838	*doll's face, punctuation*

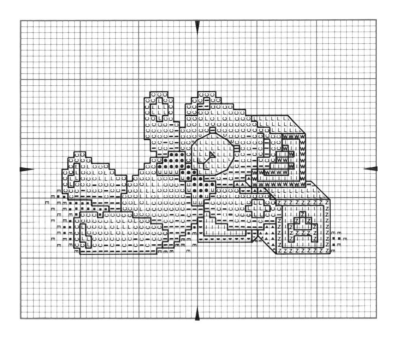

Little bear with his blocks appears in the what-not shelf on page 1, but he would also look great on a bib, shirt, or crib-pillow.

The bear and blocks were worked on aida 14 using 2 strands embroidery floss for cross-stitch and 1 strand for backstitch. Before starting, see *How Many Strands,* page 66.

Fabric	Design size	Fabric size for project shown
Aida 14	4″ × 2″	10″ × 8″

DMC Six-Strand Floss

Cross-stitch

z z	211	lavender, lt.
∧∧	223	shell pink, med.
w w	353	peach flesh
– –	407	rose brown, dk.
∩∩	543	beige-brown, ultra lt.
▲▲	632	rose brown, v. dk.
ı ı	746	off white
m m	762	pearl grey, v. lt.
◣◣	839	beige-brown, dk.
▪▪	932	antique blue, lt.
○○	950	rose brown, lt.
L L	951	rose brown, v. lt.
◣◣	955	nile green, lt.
●●	962	dusty rose, med.
u u	3687	mauve

Backstitch

	839	*all*

77

THE ROSE IS RED

Shown on page 13

The most familiar Valentine verse today is also one of the oldest. "The Rose Is Red" was first printed in 1784, but is certainly much older. The verse continues, "Thou art my love and I am thine; / I drew thee to my Valentine: / The lot was cast and then I drew, / And fortune said it shou'd be you."

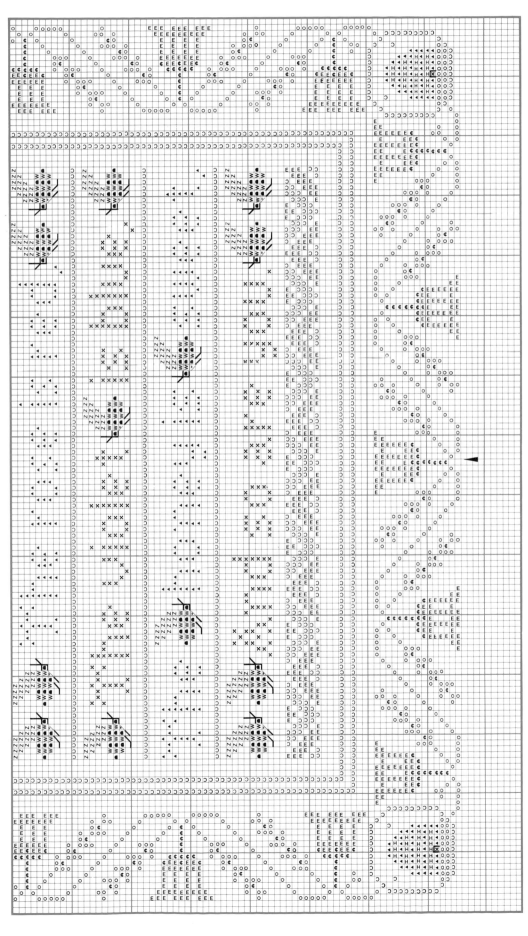

The classic floral motif, bordering this sampler, makes an elegant trim you can apply to a country basket of roses and violets (page 64).

The original design was worked on aida 14 using 3 strands embroidery floss for cross-stitch and 2 strands for backstitch. Before starting, see *How Many Strands*, page 66.

Fabric	Design size	Fabric size for project shown
Aida 11	13¾" × 18⅜"	20" × 24½"
Aida 14	10¾" × 14¾"	17" × 21"
Aida 18	8⅜" × 11⅜"	14½" × 17½"
Hardanger 22	6⅞" × 9⅜"	13" × 15½"
Linen 32 (over 2)	9⅜" × 12¾"	15½" × 19"

DMC Six-Strand Floss

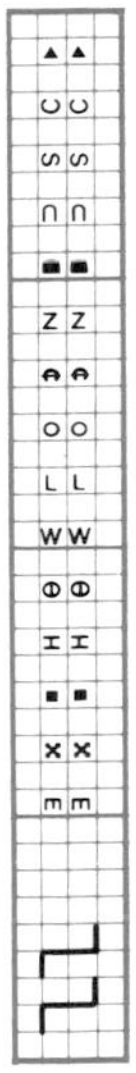

Cross-stitch

▲ ▲	223	shell pink, med.
o o	318	steel grey, lt.
s s	340	blue violet, med.
n n	341	blue violet, lt.
■ ■	414	steel grey, dk.
z z	415	pearl grey
● ●	502	blue-green
o o	503	blue-green, med.
L L	504	blue-green, lt.
w w	677	old gold, v. lt.
◎ ◎	760	salmon
⌐ ⌐	761	salmon, lt.
● ●	793	cornflower blue, med.
x x	931	antique blue, med.
m m	3042	antique violet, lt.

Backstitch

	318	*bees*
	931	*hive door*

79

YANKEE DOODLE

Shown on page 14

Yankee Doodle verses were first sung by British soldiers in the 1760's to ridicule the ragtag American armies. ("Macaroni" referred to a London fad of the time which made it popular to eat Italian macaroni and wear hairdos with large topknots called "macaronis.") Following their victory at Bunker Hill, Americans embraced the song, adding verses and making it their own.

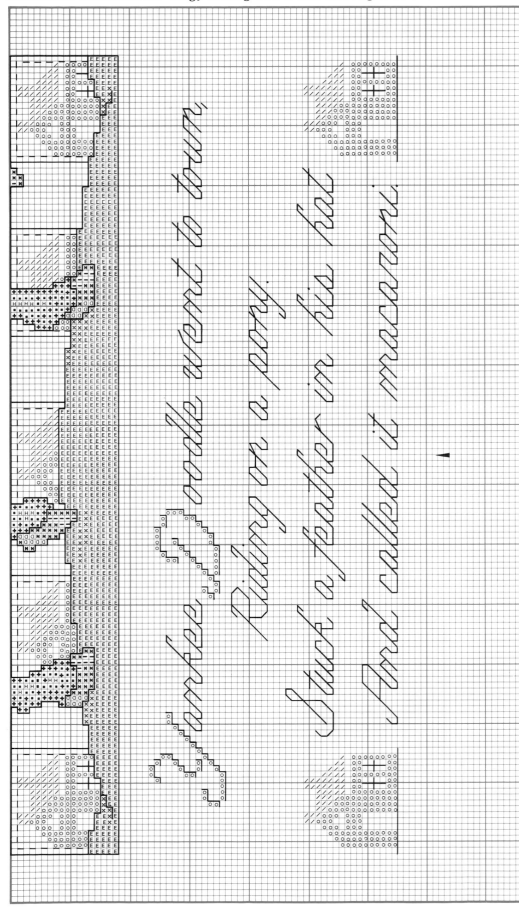

You may elect to include the verse, charted here in eighteenth-century script, or let Yankee Doodle stand on his own as he appears in the color portion of this book.

The original design was worked on aida 14 using 3 strands embroidery floss for cross-stitch and 2 strands for backstitch. Before starting, see *How Many Strands*, page 66.

Fabric	Design size	Fabric size for project shown
Aida 11	12¼″ × 16⅜″	18″ × 22″
Aida 14	9⅝″ × 13″	16″ × 19″
Aida 18	7½″ × 10″	14″ × 16″
Hardanger 22	6⅛″ × 8⅜″	12″ × 14″
Linen 32 (over 2)	8⅜″ × 11¼″	15″ × 17″

DMC Six-Strand Floss

Cross-stitch

··		white
vv		ecru
▲▲	223	shell pink, med.
∩∩	224	shell pink, lt.
ı ı	318	steel grey, lt.
⏀⏀	341	blue violet, lt.
∽∽	353	peach flesh
∧∧	402	mahogany, v. lt.
✗✗	413	pewter grey, dk.
ʊʊ	414	steel grey, dk.
●●	451	shell grey, dk.
++	452	shell grey, med.
■■	453	shell grey, lt.
◌◌	535	ash grey, v. lt.
ww	743	yellow, med.
⋰⋰	744	yellow, pale
ıı	745	yellow, lt. pale
uu	754	peach flesh, lt.
zz	758	terra cotta, lt.
∩∩	762	pearl grey, v. lt.
⊃⊃	775	baby blue, lt.
\\	778	antique mauve, lt.
▪▪	792	cornflower blue, dk.
××	793	cornflower blue, med.
⊤⊤	794	cornflower blue, lt.
mm	993	aquamarine, lt.
⊤⊤	3033	mocha brown, v. lt.
--	3064	rose brown, med.
↓↓	3328	salmon, dk.
ᴄᴄ	3705	melon, dk.
↑↑	3706	melon, med.

Cross-stitch, blended needle

◌◌	341/775	*(one strand each)*

Backstitch

	838	*figure, landscape, outer box, lettering*
	341	*background, house windows*
	341	*background*

Lazy daisy

	993	*saddle (one strand)*

French knot

·	838	*punctuation*

HEY DIDDLE, DIDDLE

Shown on page 15

Much history is said to be written between these familiar lines of nonsense. For example, "the cat" may refer to Queen Elizabeth I who was nicknamed as such for the way she toyed with her cabinet members like so many mice. She was also often seen in her private chambers, dancing in a common fashion to the music of the fiddle, which she herself played well.

When working large areas, such as silhouettes, purchase all embroidery floss from the same dye-lot. To minimize flecks of fabric showing through, pull stitches uniformly taut, but not too tight.

The original design was worked on aida 14 using 3 strands embroidery floss for cross-stitch and 2 strands for backstitch. Before starting, see *How Many Strands*, page 66.

For the complete sampler, fill the border spaces with light antique mauve (DMC 778) and eliminate border lettering.

The dish, the spoon, and the farm animals in this famous rhyme fit right into a country kitchen. The design was adapted for a pair of pot holders (page 64) backed with layers of terry cloth. Work the two designs with border lettering; eliminate the small house motif.

Fabric	Design size	Fabric size for project shown
Aida 11	13¾″ × 18⅜″	20″ × 24½″
Aida 14	10¾″ × 14¼″	17″ × 21″
Aida 18	8⅜″ × 11⅜″	14½″ × 17½″
Hardanger 22	6⅞″ × 9⅜″	13″ × 15½″
Linen 32 (over 2)	9⅜″ × 12¾″	15½″ × 19″

Pot holder fabric	Design size	Fabric size for project shown
Aida 14	5¾″ × 5¾″	10″ × 10″

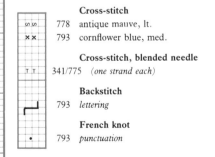

DMC Six-Strand Floss

Cross-stitch
778 antique mauve, lt.
793 cornflower blue, med.

Cross-stitch, blended needle
341/775 *(one strand each)*

Backstitch
793 *lettering*

French knot
793 *punctuation*

ONE LEAF FOR FAME

Shown on page 16

One leaf for fame, one leaf for wealth,
One for a faithful lover,
And one leaf to bring glorious health,
Are all in a four-leaf clover.

MAY BRINGS FLOCKS

LAMB BIB ꞏ Shown on page 1

When embroidering hands and faces, in order to create greater realism and expression, the backstitch line does not always run from corner to corner in the grid. Follow the chart carefully.

The original design was worked on aida 14 using 3 strands embroidery floss for cross-stitch and 2 strands for backstitch. Before starting, see *How Many Strands*, page 66.

Fabric	Design size	Fabric size for project shown
Aida 11	11¼″ × 13⅝″	17″ × 20″
Aida 14	8⅞″ × 10¾″	15″ × 17″
Aida 18	6⅞″ × 8¼″	13″ × 14″
Hardanger 22	5⅝″ × 6¾″	12″ × 13″
Linen 32 (over 2)	7¾″ × 9⅜″	14″ × 15″

DMC Six-Strand Floss

Cross-stitch

· ·		white
– –		ecru
▲ ▲	210	lavender, med.
z z	318	steel grey, lt.
n n	320	pistachio green, med.
● ●	353	peach flesh
⌒ ⌒	407	rose brown, dk.
w w	561	jade, v. dk.
ı ı	562	jade, med.
▾ ▾	563	jade, lt.
т т	564	jade, v. lt.
✦ ✦	632	rose brown, v. dk.
x x	676	old gold, lt.
■ ■	744	yellow, pale
ꞩ ꞩ	745	yellow, lt. pale
ɪ ɪ	746	off white
L L	754	peach flesh, lt.
⊕ ⊕	758	terra cotta, lt.
⊌ ⊌	760	salmon
o o	762	pearl grey, v. lt.
∧ ∧	818	baby pink
⸪ ⸪	948	peach flesh, v. lt.
u u	950	rose brown, lt.
m m	3326	rose, lt.
▲ ▲	3328	salmon, med.
т т	3348	yellow-green, lt.

Backstitch

	501	*grass, clover, flowers*
	839	*children, lettering*

French knot

•	839	*boy's eye, punctuation*

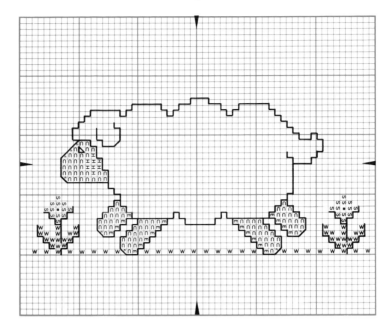

For the bib, use a ready-made terry cloth bib available at most needlework shops. The strip of aida is 14 count. Refer to alphabets 3 or 4 on page 156 depending on the length of your child's name. You may wish to use light jade (DMC 563) for a boy's name and light peach flesh (DMC 754) for a girl's name. Backstitch the lettering in dark beige-brown (DMC 839).

The lamb design was worked on aida 14 using 2 strands embroidery floss for cross-stitch and 1 strand for backstitch.

DMC Six-Strand Floss

Cross-stitch

ɪ ɪ	353	peach flesh
w w	563	jade, lt.
■ ■	744	yellow, pale
n n	754	peach flesh, lt.
m m	758	terra cotta, lt.
ꞩ ꞩ	962	dusty rose, med.

Backstitch

	839	*all art, lettering*

SING A SONG OF SIXPENCE

Shown on page 17

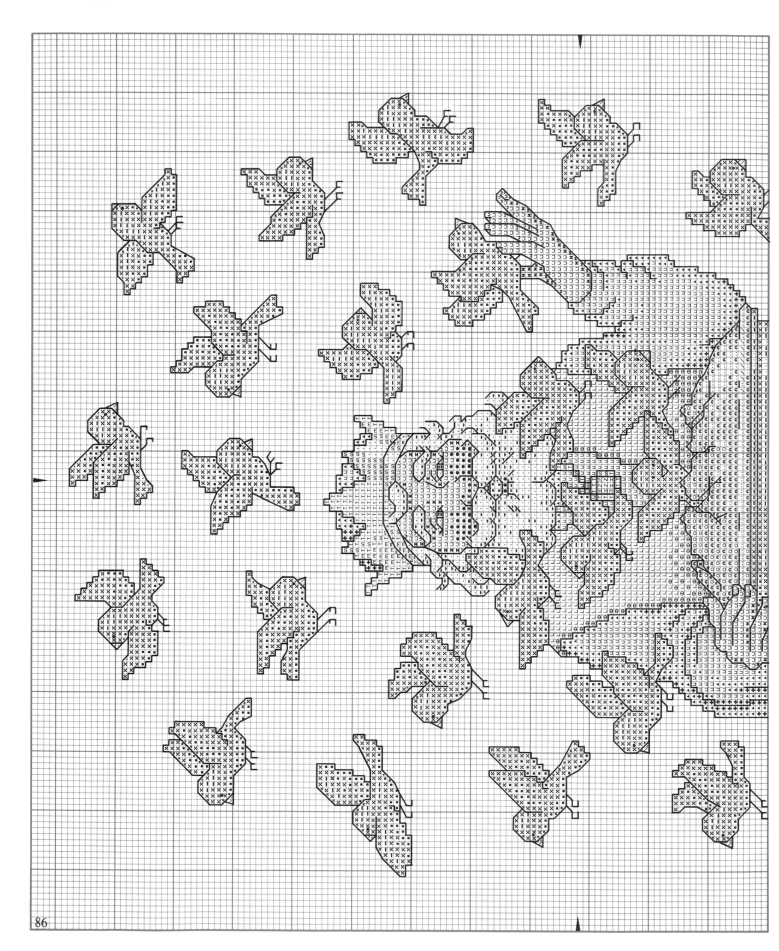

An old Italian recipe book, The Italian Banquet *(1549)*, *describes a way "to make pies so that the birds may be alive in them and flie out when it is cut up." The flutter of birds' wings would blow out the candles and stir up a pleasant commotion among the dinner guests.*

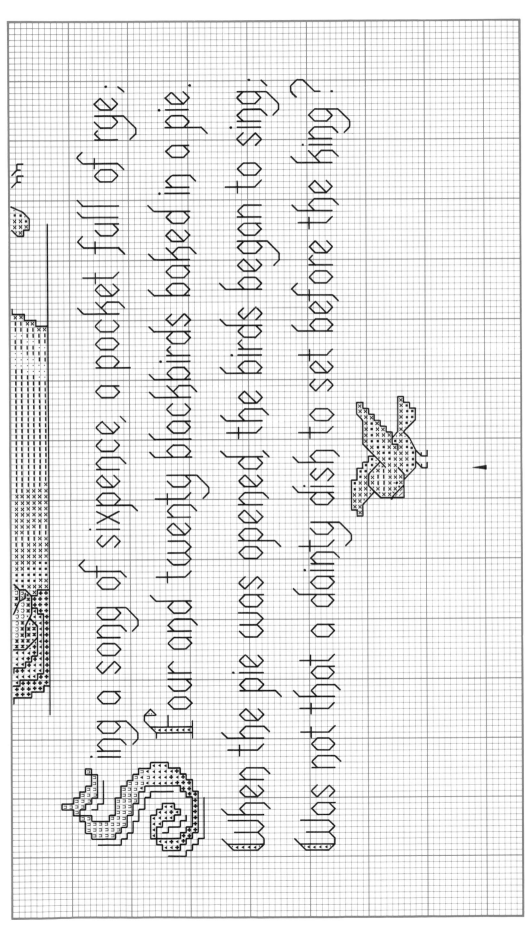

On the chart the birds are positioned more closely than they appear on page 17 to allow space for the verse.

The original design was worked on aida 14 using 3 strands embroidery floss for cross-stitch and 2 strands for backstitch. Before starting, see *How Many Strands*, page 66.

Fabric	Design size	Fabric size for project shown
Aida 11	11¾″ × 17″	18″ × 23″
Aida 14	9¼″ × 14″	15″ × 21″
Aida 18	7¼″ × 11⅜″	13″ × 17½″
Hardanger 22	5⅞″ × 9⅜″	12″ × 15½″
Linen 32 (over 2)	8⅛″ × 12¾″	14″ × 19″

DMC Six-Strand Floss

Cross-stitch

··		white
++	309	rose, deep
▲▲	335	rose
⊕⊕	340	blue violet, med.
LL	341	blue violet, lt.
●●	353	peach flesh
○○	402	mahogany, v. lt.
■■	535	ash grey, v. lt.
××	647	beaver grey, med.
⊤⊤	676	old gold, lt.
ꙅꙅ	677	old gold, v. lt.
ᵐᵐ	680	old gold, dk.
//	712	cream
\\	743	yellow, med.
○○	754	peach flesh, lt.
ꭕꭕ	758	terra cotta, lt.
▪▪	760	salmon
◆◆	793	cornflower blue, med.
∨∨	822	beige-grey, lt.
◠◠	945	rose brown
····	951	rose brown, v. lt.
ɪɪ	991	aquamarine, dk.
zz	993	aquamarine, lt.
--	3024	brown-grey, v. lt.
✗✗	3064	rose brown, med.
∪∪	3326	rose, lt.

Backstitch

	535	*birds, music*
	839	*king, pie, lettering*
	3064	*birds' legs*

French knot

·	310	*birds' eyes*
·	839	*punctuation*

There Was a Crooked Man

WELCOME SIGN ⬩ Shown on page 64

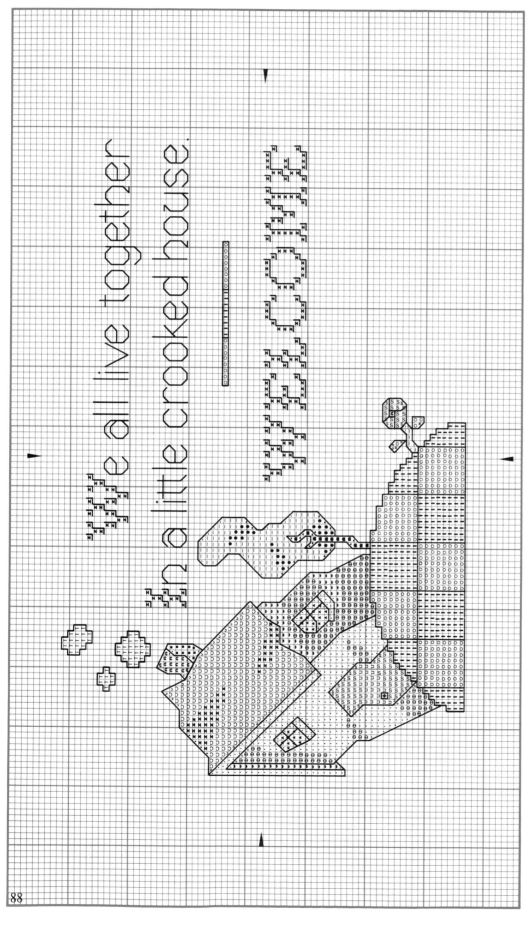

This simple adaptation of a familiar verse is the perfect way to greet your house guests and apologize for the mess, all without saying a word.

The welcome sign was worked on aida 14 using 2 strands embroidery floss for cross-stitch and 1 strand for backstitch.

Fabric	Design size	Fabric size for project shown
Aida 14	8″ × 5¼″	14″ × 11″

DMC Six-Strand Floss

Cross-stitch

		white
	352	coral, lt.
	353	peach flesh
	407	rose brown, dk.
	415	pearl grey
	564	jade, v. lt.
	676	old gold, lt.
	712	cream
	744	yellow, pale
	746	off white
	762	pearl grey, v. lt.
	794	cornflower blue, lt.
	807	peacock blue
	962	dusty rose, med.
	992	aquamarine
	993	aquamarine, lt.
	3326	rose, lt.

Backstitch

	838	*all*

French knot

	838	*punctuation*

SEE A PIN

Shown on page 18

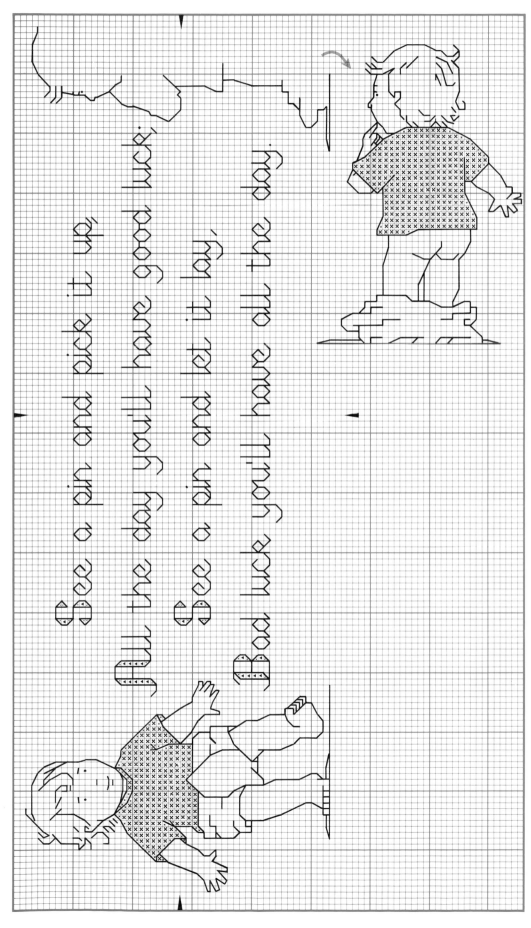

The line for the babies does not always follow the grid from corner to corner. It was designed to resemble a freestyle line drawing. Follow the chart carefully.

Instead of stitching safety pins, substitute brass or rustproof safety pins (page 1). Sew them on the background fabric concealing the stitches at the head and loop of the pins.

The original design was worked on aida 14 using 2 strands embroidery floss for cross-stitch and 1 strand for backstitch. Before starting, see *How Many Strands*, page 66.

Fabric	Design size	Fabric size for project shown
Aida 11	15" × 5½"	21" × 12"
Aida 14	11¾" × 4¼"	18" × 10"
Linen 32 (over 2)	10¼" × 3¾"	16" × 10"

DMC Six-Strand Floss

Cross-stitch

× ×	745	yellow, lt. pale
▲ ▲	776	pink, med.

Backstitch

322	*lettering*
838	*babies*

French knot

322	*punctuation*
838	*babies' eyes*

DAFFY-DOWN-DILLY

Shown on page 19

The daffodil, emblem of Wales, symbol of unrequited love, heraldic symbol of courage, chivalry, and esteem, means something much simpler to most of us— Spring has arrived!

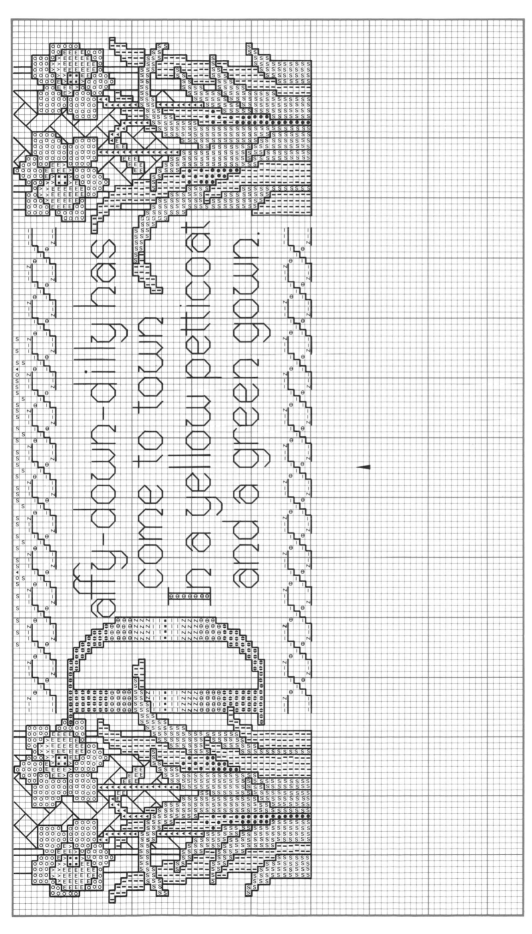

When embroidering hands and faces, in order to create greater realism and expression, the backstitch line does not always run from corner to corner in the grid. Follow the chart carefully.

When working large areas, such as the dress, purchase all embroidery floss from the same dye-lot. To minimize flecks of fabric showing through, pull stitches uniformly taut, but not too tight.

The original design was worked on aida 14 using 3 strands embroidery floss for cross-stitch and 2 strands (or 1 strand as noted) for backstitch. Before starting, see *How Many Strands*, page 66.

Fabric	Design size	Fabric size for project shown
Aida 11	13¼″ × 15½″	19″ × 22″
Aida 14	10⅜″ × 12⅛″	16½″ × 18″
Aida 18	8″ × 9⅜″	14″ × 15½″
Hardanger 22	6⅝″ × 7¾″	12½″ × 14″
Linen 32 (over 2)	9⅛″ × 10⅞″	15″ × 17″

DMC Six-Strand Floss

Cross-stitch

		white
∩ ∩	211	lavender, lt.
● ●	341	blue violet, lt.
▪ ▪	353	peach flesh
+ +	407	rose brown, dk.
w w	543	beige-brown, ultra lt.
† †	676	old gold, lt.
L L	712	cream
v v	742	tangerine, lt.
m m	743	yellow, med.
∧ ∧	744	yellow, pale
o o	745	yellow, lt. pale
x x	754	peach flesh, lt.
∴ ∴	758	terra cotta, lt.
⊠ ⊠	899	rose, med.
T T	948	peach flesh, v. lt.
⊙ ⊙	950	rose brown, lt.
◡ ◡	951	rose brown, v. lt.
∽ ∽	955	nile green, lt.
⊕ ⊕	961	dusty rose, dk.
● ●	991	aquamarine, dk.
I I	992	aquamarine
▲ ▲	993	aquamarine, lt.
u u	3326	rose, lt.
– –	3341	apricot
◑ ◑	3687	mauve
z z	3706	melon, med.

Backstitch

	838	*girl, daffodils*
	840	*lattice, spiral border design (1 strand)*
	991	*large D, lettering*

French knot

•	353	*daffodils in girl's hand*
•	991	*punctuation*

RAIN, RAIN, GO AWAY

Shown on page 21

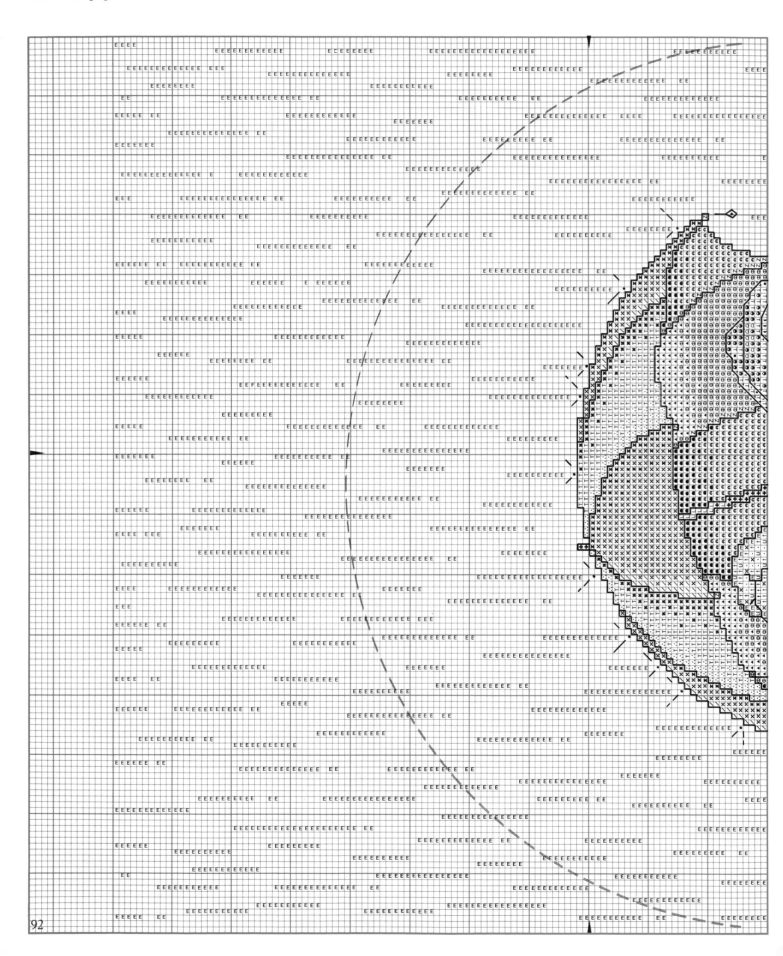

There are many variations on the theme of "rain, rain, go away," including a curse, "Rain, rain, go away,/Come on Mary's wedding day."

The original design was worked on aida 14 using 3 strands embroidery floss for cross-stitch and 2 strands for backstitch. Before starting, see *How Many Strands*, page 66.

Frame this scene with an arched mat as indicated by the dotted line at the top of the pattern. Do not stitch the arch outline; it is placed as a guide only.

Fabric	Design size	Fabric size for project shown
Aida 11	13¼″ × 16½″	19″ × 22″
Aida 14	10½″ × 13″	17″ × 20″
Aida 18	8¼″ × 10″	14″ × 16″
Hardanger 22	6⅝″ × 8¼″	13″ × 14″
Linen 32 (over 2)	9⅛″ × 11¼″	15″ × 17″

DMC Six-Strand Floss

Cross-stitch

· ·		white
x x	209	lavender, dk.
x x	210	lavender, med.
/ /	211	lavender, lt.
ı ı	221	shell pink, dk.
◆ ◆	309	rose, deep
▲ ▲	333	blue violet, dk.
⊕ ⊕	340	blue violet, med.
ʌ ʌ	341	blue violet, lt.
▷ ▷	353	peach flesh
c c	369	pistachio green, v. lt.
L L	407	rose brown, dk.
« «	738	tan, v. lt.
ఠ ఠ	744	yellow, pale
I I	745	yellow, lt. pale
▽ ▽	746	off white
\ \	754	peach flesh, lt.
✦ ✦	758	terra cotta, lt.
ɪ ɪ	775	baby blue, lt.
u u	776	pink, med.
■ ■	792	cornflower blue, dk.
ʌ ʌ	793	cornflower blue, med.
z z	794	cornflower blue, lt.
⧫ ⧫	797	royal blue
▾ ▾	798	delft, dk.
ı ı	799	delft, med.
m m	800	delft, pale
∴ ∴	818	baby pink
u u	945	rose brown
v v	950	rose brown, lt.
w w	962	dusty rose, med.
■ ■	3022	brown-grey, med.
⊥ ⊥	3023	brown-grey, lt.
⊙ ⊙	3024	brown-grey, v. lt.
⊖ ⊖	3033	mocha brown, v. lt.
● ●	3687	mauve
✗ ✗	3688	mauve, med.
⊤ ⊤	3689	mauve, lt.
○ ○	3708	melon, lt.

Backstitch

	798	*rain splashes, drips, puddles*
	902	*children, umbrellas, boat, doll*

French knot

·	798	*rain*
·	902	*doll, doll umbrella*

ONE, TWO, BUCKLE MY SHOE

Shown on page 23

One, Two, Buckle My Shoe originally counted up to, ". . . Twenty nine, the game is mine;/Thirty, thirty, make a kerchy." Many old verses known to us today are mere fragments of otherwise long-forgotten songs. Andrew Lang, a noted 19th-century editor, once described nursery rhymes as "smooth stones from the brook of time, worn round by constant friction of tongues long silent."

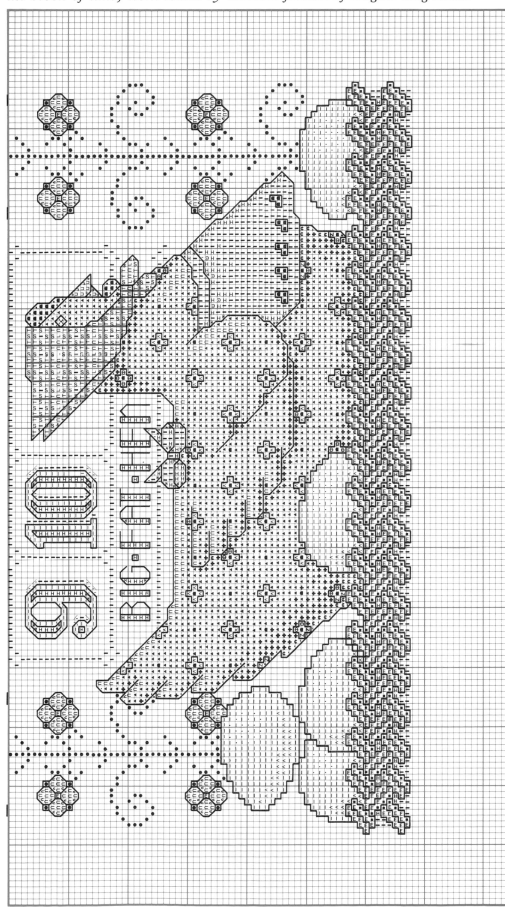

The original design was worked on aida 14 using 3 strands embroidery floss for cross-stitch and 2 strands for backstitch. Before starting, see *How Many Strands*, page 66.

Fabric	Design size	Fabric size for project shown
Aida 11	11¾" × 16¼"	18" × 22"
Aida 14	9¼" × 12⅞"	15" × 19"
Aida 18	7¼" × 10"	13" × 16"
Hardanger 22	5⅞" × 8¼"	12" × 14"
Linen 32 (over 2)	8⅛" × 11¼"	14" × 17"

DMC Six-Strand Floss

Cross-stitch

. .		white
+ +	223	shell pink, med.
n n	315	antique mauve, dk.
ω ω	369	pistachio green, v. lt.
z z	407	rose brown, dk.
■ ■	422	hazel nut brown, lt.
L L	554	violet, lt.
- -	632	rose brown, v. dk.
⌐ ⌐	712	cream
u u	743	yellow, med.
m m	744	yellow, pale
T T	745	yellow, lt. pale
▲ ▲	760	salmon
⋂ ⋂	761	salmon, lt.
⊙ ⊙	792	cornflower blue, dk.
I I	793	cornflower blue, med.
I I	794	cornflower blue, lt.
w w	839	beige-brown, dk.
Φ Φ	950	rose brown, lt.
∧ ∧	951	rose brown, v. lt.
● ●	992	aquamarine
○ ○	993	aquamarine, lt.
■ ■	3350	dusty rose, v. dk.

Backstitch

	223	*inside scarf*
	902	*all art, lettering*

French knot

·	white	*highlight in hen's eye*
·	902	*little hen's eyes and feet*

ONE, HE LOVES

Shown on page 24

When working large areas, such as silhouettes, purchase all embroidery floss from the same dye-lot. To minimize flecks of fabric showing through, pull stitches uniformly taut, but not too tight.

The original design was worked on aida 14 using 3 strands embroidery floss for cross-stitch and 2 strands for backstitch. Before starting, see *How Many Strands*, page 66.

Fabric	Design size	Fabric size for project shown
Aida 11	11¾″ × 8¼″	18″ × 14″
Aida 14	9¼″ × 6½″	15″ × 12″
Aida 18	7¼″ × 5″	13″ × 11″
Hardanger 22	5⅞″ × 4¼″	12″ × 10″
Linen 32 (over 2)	8⅛″ × 5⅝″	14″ × 11½″

DMC Six-Strand Floss

Cross-stitch

··		white
⊕⊕	318	steel grey, lt.
∩∩	351	coral
✦✦	352	coral, lt.
II	353	peach flesh
⊙⊙	407	rose brown, dk.
■■	436	tan
LL	437	tan, lt.
≎≎	501	blue-green, dk.
vv	502	blue-green
▲▲	504	blue-green, lt.
◐◐	632	rose brown, v. dk.
∧∧	738	tan, v. lt.
☉☉	739	tan, ultra lt.
TT	744	yellow, pale
mm	745	yellow, lt. pale

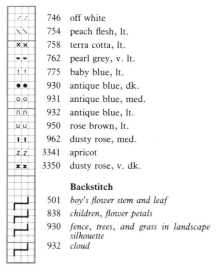

·.·.	746	off white
\\\\	754	peach flesh, lt.
××	758	terra cotta, lt.
--	762	pearl grey, v. lt.
⌐t⌐t	775	baby blue, lt.
●●	930	antique blue, dk.
○○	931	antique blue, med.
∩∩	932	antique blue, lt.
∪∪	950	rose brown, lt.
II	962	dusty rose, med.
zz	3341	apricot
xx	3350	dusty rose, v. dk.

Backstitch

	501	*boy's flower stem and leaf*
	838	*children, flower petals*
	930	*fence, trees, and grass in landscape silhouette*
	932	*cloud*

I Bought a Dozen New-Laid Eggs

Shown on page 20 ❧ (instructions on page 98)

I bought a dozen new-laid eggs,
Of good old farmer Dickens;
I hobbled home upon two legs,
And found them full of chickens.

CACKLE, CACKLE

Shown on page 22

The original design was worked on aida 14 using 3 strands embroidery floss for cross-stitch and 2 strands for backstitch. Before starting, see *How Many Strands*, page 66.

Fabric	Design size	Fabric size for project shown
Aida 11	11¼" × 13⅝"	17" × 20"
Aida 14	8⅞" × 10¾"	15" × 17"
Aida 18	6⅞" × 8¼"	13" × 14"
Hardanger 22	5⅝" × 6¾"	12" × 13"
Linen 32 (over 2)	7¾" × 9⅜"	14" × 15"

DMC Six-Strand Floss

Cross-stitch

· ·		white
x x	333	blue violet, dk.
I I	340	blue violet, med.
ʊ ʊ	341	blue violet, lt.
◌ ◌	352	coral, lt.
L L	353	peach flesh
▲ ▲	407	rose brown, dk.
H H	415	pearl grey
∽ ∽	543	beige-brown, ultra lt.
■ ■	562	jade, med.
⦂⦂	563	jade, lt.
∩ ∩	564	jade, v. lt.
● ●	632	rose brown, v. dk.
/ /	712	cream
Φ Φ	743	yellow, med.
o o	745	yellow, lt. pale
t t	762	pearl grey, v. lt.
∧ ∧	776	pink, med.
w w	793	cornflower blue, med.
u u	800	delft, pale
= =	818	baby pink
● ●	930	antique blue, dk.
− −	945	rose brown
⊙ ⊙	950	rose brown, lt.
m m	951	rose brown, v. lt.
x x	962	dusty rose, med.
+ +	3687	mauve
∩ ∩	3688	mauve, med.
⌄ ⌄	3708	melon, lt.

Backstitch

	840	*barn, house, shrubs, grass, flowers*
	902	*bunny, basket, eggs, lettering*

French knot

•	902	*punctuation*

Create a personalized pillow for your sleepyhead (page 1).

See alphabet 10, page 157. For a girl's name you might wish to use medium shell pink (DMC 223), and for a boy's name consider light cornflower blue (DMC 794). Backstitch outlines of names in dark beige-brown (DMC 839).

When embroidering hands and faces, in order to create greater realism and expression, the backstitch line does not always run from corner to corner in the grid. Follow the chart carefully.

The original design was worked on aida 14 using 3 strands embroidery floss for cross-stitch and 2 strands for backstitch. Before starting, see *How Many Strands*, page 66.

Fabric	Design size	Fabric size for project shown
Aida 14	11" × 9"	17" × 17"

DMC Six-Strand Floss

Cross-stitch

· ·		white
w w	223	shell pink, med.
▲ ▲	315	antique mauve, dk.
⇄ ⇄	317	pewter grey
■ ■	318	steel grey, lt.
∩ ∩	353	peach flesh
Φ Φ	415	pearl grey
+ +	435	brown, v. lt.
I I	437	tan, lt.
− −	712	cream
v v	738	tan, v. lt.
T T	739	tan, ultra lt.
o o	754	peach flesh, lt.
m m	758	terra cotta, lt.
∽ ∽	760	salmon
ⲓ ⲓ	761	salmon, lt.
L L	762	pearl grey, v. lt.
● ●	792	cornflower blue, dk.
▲ ▲	793	cornflower blue, med.
u u	794	cornflower blue, lt.
x x	841	beige-brown, lt.
∩ ∩	842	beige-brown, v. lt.
\ \	948	peach flesh, v. lt.

Backstitch

	839	*child, pillow, feathers*
	841	*feather details*

*Who was Mother Goose? Some historians point to "goose-footed Bertha,"
thought to be the mother of the emperor Charlemagne, so named because of a
deformity of her foot. French legendry depicts her as spinning while telling tales
to a gathering of children.*

Shown on page 25

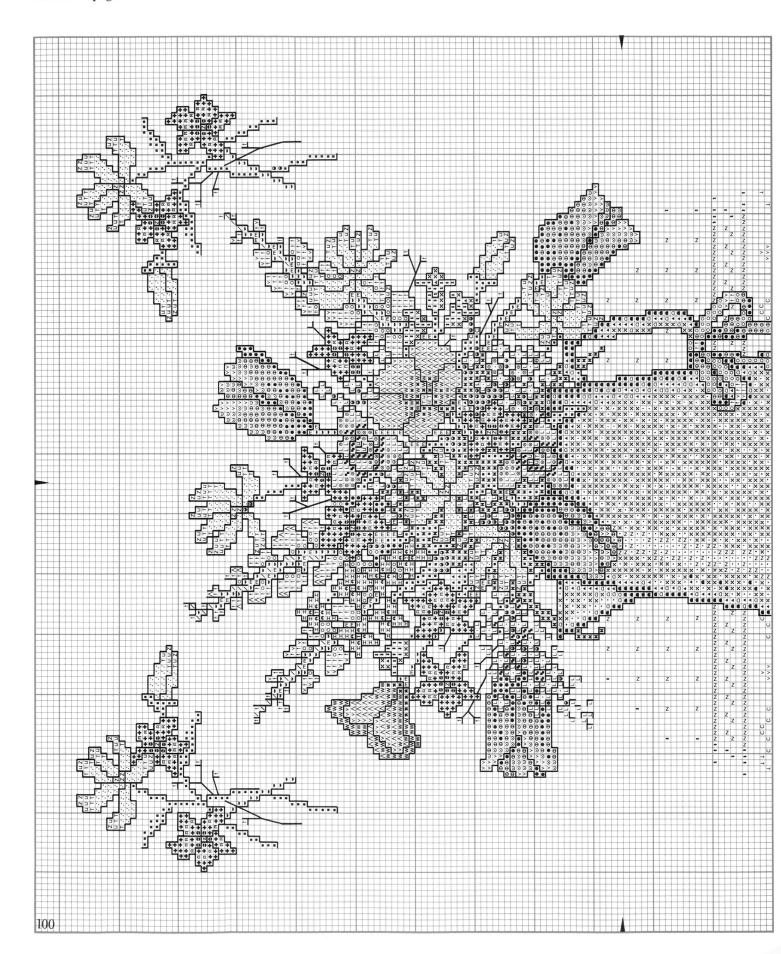

There was a time when the May Pole was as tall as a ship's mast raised in front of the village church. Folks went to the woods and returned laden with flowers and green boughs. It was said they "brought home the May." Wreaths were hung from the pole and everyone danced rings around it all day.

Keep the design together in one sampler, or make the frame and towel set shown on page 64. Towels and frames are available in most needlework shops.

The original design was worked on aida 14 using 3 strands embroidery floss for cross-stitch and 2 strands for backstitch. The towel was worked with 2 strand cross-stitch and 1 strand backstitch. Before starting, see *How Many Strands*, page 66.

Fabric	Design size	Fabric size for project shown
Aida 11	12¾″ × 16½″	19″ × 23″
Aida 14	10″ × 13″	16″ × 19″
Aida 18	7¾″ × 10″	14″ × 16″
Hardanger 22	6⅜″ × 8¼″	12″ × 14″
Linen 32 (over 2)	8¾″ × 11¼″	15″ × 17″

DMC Six-Strand Floss

Cross-stitch

··		white
⅍⅍	208	lavender, v. dk.
⊙⊙	209	lavender, dk.
ᒻᒻ	211	lavender, lt.
●●	309	rose, deep
⅀⅀	317	pewter grey
◠◠	318	steel grey, lt.
≎≎	333	blue violet, dk.
⊕⊕	335	rose
++	340	blue violet, med.
ᴙᴙ	341	blue violet, lt.
ᴜᴜ	353	peach flesh
ᴍᴍ	367	pistachio green, dk.
◡◡	368	pistachio green, lt.
∕∕	369	pistachio green, v. lt.
ʜʜ	561	jade, v. dk.
⚇⚇	562	jade, med.
■■	563	jade, lt.
ᴄᴄ	564	jade, v. lt.
ᴛᴛ	744	yellow, pale
⅃⅃	747	sky blue, v. lt.
＼＼	754	peach flesh, lt.
ᴡᴡ	760	salmon
ᴧᴧ	761	salmon, lt.
ᴕᴕ	762	pearl grey, v. lt.
ɪɪ	775	baby blue, lt.
꜔꜔	776	pink, med.
▴▴	797	royal blue
ᴀᴀ	798	delft, dk.
xx	799	delft, med.
ɴɴ	800	delft, pale
ᴠᴠ	818	baby pink
ɢɢ	838	beige-brown, v. dk.
⊙⊙	962	dusty rose, med.
∴∴	3078	golden yellow, v. lt.
✕✕	3328	salmon, med.
ᴢᴢ	3341	apricot
⊕⊕	3607	plum, lt.
ɪɪ	3609	plum, ultra lt.
⊛⊛	3708	melon, lt.

Backstitch

	562	*baby's breath stems (1 strand)*
	838	*all other backstitch*

THE FAIR MAID

Shown on page 27

In ages past, the hawthorn tree was believed to be holy, a landmark where spirits gathered. It was planted at crossroads, also thought to be sites where spirits met. Cutting a blossom was bad luck but tieing a ribbon or length of cloth to a branch brought good luck.

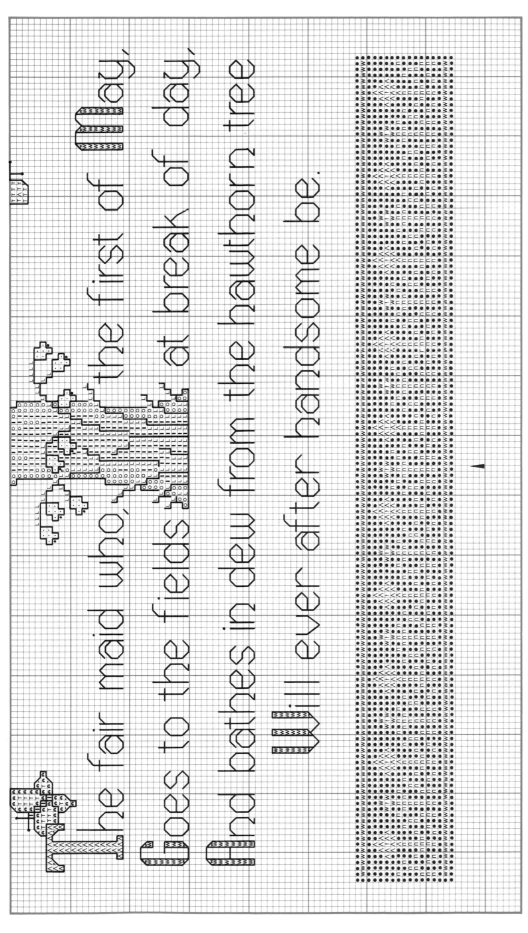

The original design was worked on aida 14 using 3 strands embroidery floss for cross-stitch and 2 strands for backstitch. Before starting, see *How Many Strands,* page 66.

Fabric	Design size	Fabric size for project shown
Aida 11	12¾″ × 17¾″	19″ × 24″
Aida 14	10″ × 14″	16″ × 20″
Aida 18	7¾″ × 10¾″	14″ × 17″
Hardanger 22	6⅜″ × 8⅞″	12″ × 15″
Linen 32 (over 2)	8¾″ × 12⅛″	15″ × 18″

DMC Six-Strand Floss

Cross-stitch

✷✷	322	navy blue, v. lt.
▪▪	335	rose
▫▫	351	coral
N N	353	peach flesh
▾▾	501	blue-green, dk.
∩ ∩	502	blue-green
L L	503	blue-green, med.
\ \	504	blue-green, lt.
▪▪	553	violet, med.
W W	554	violet, lt.
· ·	712	cream
u u	744	yellow, pale
T T	745	yellow, lt. pale
t t	746	off white
v v	754	peach flesh, lt.
∩ ∩	818	baby pink
o o	840	beige-brown, med.
I I	841	beige-brown, lt.
+ +	842	beige-brown, v. lt.
ω ω	899	rose, med.
●●	930	antique blue, dk.
/ /	948	peach flesh, v. lt.
· ·	961	dusty rose, dk.
m m	962	dusty rose, med.
⊥ ⊥	3046	yellow beige, med.
∧ ∧	3326	rose, lt.
M M	3341	apricot
Φ Φ	3708	melon, lt.

Backstitch

	930	*all*

French knot

·	744	*flowers*
·	930	*birds, girl, punctuation*

THE COCK CROWS

Shown on page 26

BIRDS OF A FEATHER

Shown on page 28

The original design was worked on aida 14 using 3 strands embroidery floss for cross-stitch and 2 strands for backstitch. Before starting, see *How Many Strands,* page 66.

Fabric	Design size	Fabric size for project shown
Aida 11	13¾″ × 9½″	20″ × 15″
Aida 14	10¾″ × 7¼″	17″ × 13″
Aida 18	8⅜″ × 5½″	14½″ × 11½″
Hardanger 22	6⅞″ × 4½″	13″ × 10½″
Linen 32 (over 2)	9⅜″ × 6¼″	15½″ × 12″

DMC Six-Strand Floss

Cross-stitch

· ·		white
x x	312	navy blue, lt.
■ ■	318	steel grey, lt.
I I	322	navy blue, v. lt.
▲ ▲	334	baby blue, med.
w w	353	peach flesh
● ●	407	rose brown, dk.
⊙ ⊙	415	pearl grey
∽ ∽	437	tan, lt.
+ +	632	rose brown, v. dk.
✕ ✕	676	old gold, lt.
– –	712	cream
z z	738	tan, v. lt.
u u	739	tan, ultra lt.
θ θ	743	yellow, med.
t t	744	yellow, pale
H H	746	off white
⋰⋰	754	peach flesh, lt.
▴ ▴	758	terra cotta, lt.
◡ ◡	762	pearl grey, v. lt.
⊥ ⊥	775	baby blue, lt.
т т	776	pink, med.
ˡ ˡ	948	peach flesh, v. lt.
Φ Φ	950	rose brown, lt.
m m	956	geranium
o o	957	geranium, pale
✕ ✕	961	dusty rose, dk.
n n	3325	baby blue
● ●	3350	dusty rose, v. dk.
△ △	3705	melon, dk.

Backstitch

	356	*cock's legs (3 strands)*
	838	*all other backstitch*

French knot

·	838	*cock, teddy bear, punctuation*

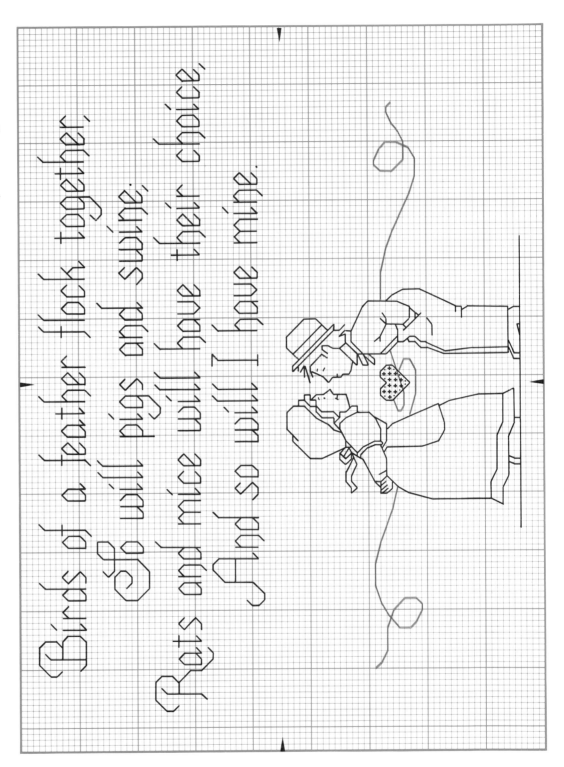

The original design was worked on aida 14 using 2 strands embroidery floss for cross-stitch and 1 strand for backstitch.

Fabric	Design size	Fabric size for project shown
Aida 11	11″ × 8¼″	17″ × 14″
Aida 14	8½″ × 6½″	15″ × 13″
Linen 32 (over 2)	7½″ × 5⅝″	14″ × 12″

DMC Six-Strand Floss

Cross-stitch

+ +	3708	melon, lt.

Backstitch

	312	*line that loops heart*
	902	*all other backstitch*

French knot

·	902	*punctuation*

HEARTS LIKE DOORS

Shown on page 29

Early-American educators demanded students be instructed in polite conversation and correct manners. Rudeness in the classroom could result in the guilty student being pinned to the mistress' apron. Stern rules for living, often presented in verse form, filled the textbooks. Occasionally, similar rhymes found their way into Mother Goose editions.

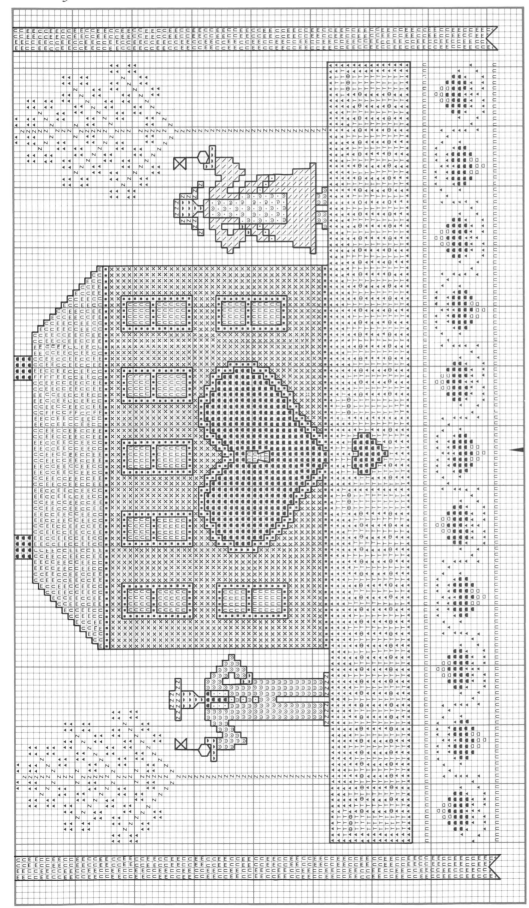

The original design was worked on aida 14 using 3 strands embroidery floss for cross-stitch and 2 strands for backstitch. Before starting, see *How Many Strands*, page 66.

Fabric	Design size	Fabric size for project shown
Aida 11	13″ × 18¼″	19″ × 24″
Aida 14	10¼″ × 14¾″	16″ × 21″
Aida 18	7⅞″ × 11⅜″	14″ × 17″
Hardanger 22	6½″ × 9⅜″	12″ × 15″
Linen 32 (over 2)	9⅛″ × 12⅞″	15″ × 19″

DMC Six-Strand Floss

Cross-stitch

· ·			white
z z	407	rose brown, dk.
m m	415	pearl grey
Φ Φ	543	beige-brown, ultra lt.
■ ■	712	cream
\ \	743	yellow, med.
т т	746	off white
∽ ∽	754	peach flesh, lt.
n n	793	cornflower blue, med.
x x	794	cornflower blue, lt.
● ●	899	rose, med.
▲ ▲	958	seagreen, dk.
ʊ ʊ	3341	apricot
◻ ◻	3708	melon, lt.

Backstitch

	414	*keys*
	792	*lettering*
	793	*all other backstitch*

French knot

·	792	*punctuation*

To complement the sampler, portions of the design can be applied to placemats, napkins, and a bread cover (see pattern, page 108). These items are available in most needlework and craft stores.

The table set was worked on ready-made covers of 14-count oatmeal colored aida. Two strands embroidery floss were used for cross-stitch and 1 strand for backstitch.

For napkins, sew the corner design with five large berries. Work the borders six counts in from the hemline and extend them all the way around. The corner bird is optional for napkins.

For the bread cover, sew the corner design with nine large berries and the bird in the corner. Work the borders six counts in from the fabric hemline and extend them all the way around.

For placemats, work the borders six counts within the fabric hemline. Repeat the two left-side corners in mirror-image on the right side and connect the borders. Center the pair of birds within the inner border.

HEARTS LIKE DOORS

TABLE SET ● Shown on page 64 (instructions on page 107)

Top left-side placemat corner
and napkin corner

Bread cover corner design

Bottom left-side placemat corner

GOOD, BETTER, BEST

Shown on page 30

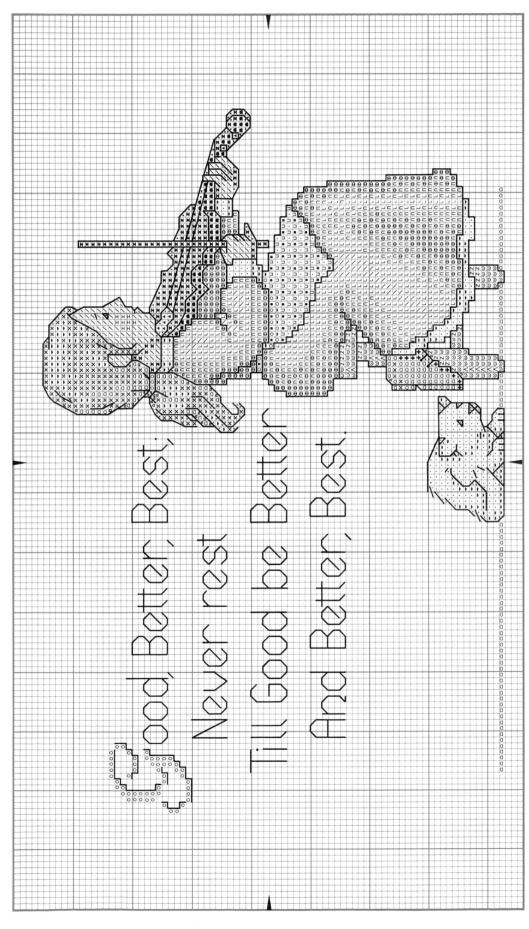

The original design was worked on aida 14 using 3 strands embroidery floss for cross-stitch and 2 strands for backstitch. Before starting, see *How Many Strands*, page 66.

Fabric	Design size	Fabric size for project shown
Aida 11	11" × 7¾"	17" × 14"
Aida 14	8⅝" × 6⅛"	15" × 12"
Aida 18	6⅝" × 4¾"	13" × 11"
Linen 32 (over 2)	7½" × 5⅜"	14" × 12"

DMC Six-Strand Floss

Cross-stitch

··		white
⊡⊡	353	peach flesh
▪▪	356	terra cotta, med.
◧◧	407	rose brown, dk.
ᴢᴢ	435	brown, v. lt.
ᵕᵕ	437	tan, lt.
▲▲	535	ash grey, v. lt.
--	543	beige-brown, ultra lt.
++	632	rose brown, v. dk.
◎◎	676	old gold, lt.
∧∧	738	tan, v. lt.
∩∩	744	yellow, pale
ʟʟ	745	yellow, lt. pale
＼＼	746	off white
∕∕	754	peach flesh, lt.
✖✖	758	terra cotta, lt.
××	950	rose brown, lt.
▪▪	3705	melon, dk.
○○	3706	melon, med.
ᵁᵁ	3708	melon, lt.

Backstitch

	543	*fiddle strings*
	839	*all other backstitch*

French knot

·	839	*punctuation*

MARY MARY, QUITE CONTRARY

Shown on page 31

Tommy Thumb's Pretty Song Book *(c. 1744) is the earliest surviving nursery rhyme book. Among the thirty-eight classic verses appearing in it are "Mary, Mary" (or "Mistress Mary"), "Sing a Song of Sixpence," "Hickory, Dickory, Dock," and "Bah, Bah, Black Sheep." The book measured less than two by three inches.*

The original design was worked on aida 14 using 3 strands embroidery floss for cross-stitch and 2 strands for backstitch. Before starting, see *How Many Strands*, page 66.

Fabric	Design size	Fabric size for project shown
Aida 11	12¾″ × 18″	19″ × 24″
Aida 14	10″ × 14⅜″	16″ × 20″
Aida 18	7¾″ × 11″	14″ × 17″
Hardanger 22	6⅜″ × 9⅛″	12″ × 15″
Linen 32 (over 2)	8¾″ × 12½″	15″ × 18″

DMC Six-Strand Floss

Cross-stitch

· ·		white
◡ ◡	211	lavender, lt.
s s	320	pistachio green, med.
◠ ◠	335	rose
▲ ▲	340	blue violet, med.
◣ ◣	353	peach flesh
ı ı	368	pistachio green, lt.
◔ ◔	402	mahogany, v. lt.
■ ■	415	pearl grey
● ●	501	blue-green, dk.
○ ○	503	blue-green, med.
◼ ◼	561	jade, v. dk.
× ×	563	jade, lt.
w w	676	old gold, lt.
˙·	712	cream
ʟ ʟ	744	yellow, pale
ɪ ɪ	745	yellow, lt. pale
n n	746	off white
＼ ＼	754	peach flesh, lt.
◖ ◖	758	terra cotta, lt.
† †	775	baby blue, lt.
✛ ✛	813	blue, lt.
◡ ◡	818	baby pink
⊠ ⊠	826	blue, med.
◉ ◉	827	blue, v. lt.
◡ ◡	828	blue, ultra lt.
⌃ ⌃	842	beige-brown, v. lt.
m m	927	grey-green, med.
∧ ∧	962	dusty rose, med.
v v	3072	beaver grey, v. lt.
◎ ◎	3341	apricot
ɴ ɴ	3706	melon, med.

Backstitch

⌐	501	*flower stems in Mary's hand and in garden rows*
⌐	826	*water droplets*
⌐	838	*all other backstitch*

French knot

·	838	*punctuation*

WINTER, SPRING, SUMMER, AUTUMN

Shown on pages 32–33

112

Weather is a universal language, and few people can begin a conversation without it. Some notable examples are "When it is evening, ye say, it will be fair weather for the sky is red" (Matthew 16:2), "Everyone talks about the weather, but nobody does anything about it" (Mark Twain), and "A sunshiny shower won't last half an hour" (Mother Goose).

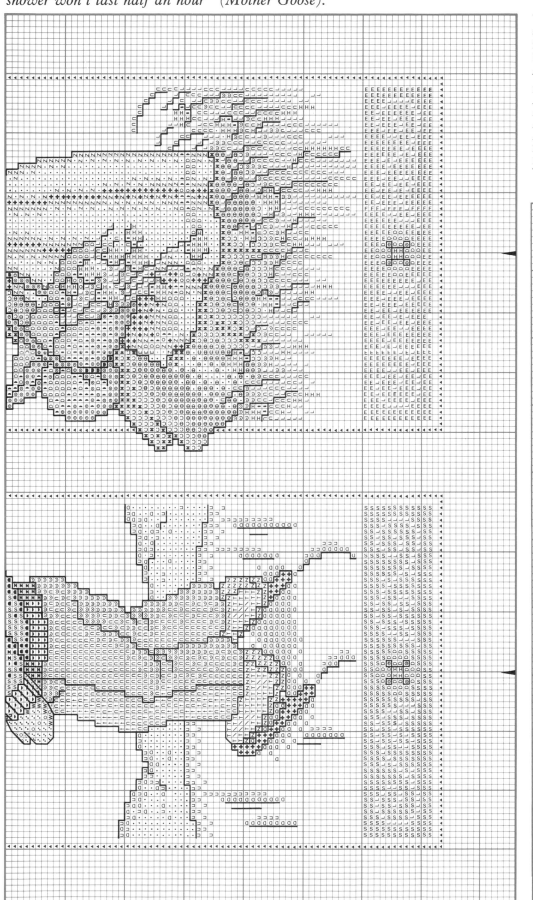

The original design was worked on aida 14 using 3 strands embroidery floss for cross-stitch and 2 strands for backstitch. Before starting, see *How Many Strands*, page 66.

Fabric	Design size	Fabric size
	(for each individual season)	
Aida 11	5½" × 17¼"	12" × 23"
Aida 14	4⅜" × 13½"	10" × 19½"
Aida 18	3⅜" × 10½"	9½" × 16½"
Hardanger 22	2¾" × 8⅝"	9" × 14½"
Linen 32 (over 2)	3¾" × 11⅞"	10" × 18"

DMC Six-Strand Floss

Cross-stitch

· ·		white
m m	208	lavender, v. dk.
н н	209	lavender, dk.
o o	210	lavender, med.
⊕ ⊕	211	lavender, lt.
✦ ✦	318	steel grey, lt.
ς ς	340	blue violet, med.
∩ ∩	341	blue violet, lt.
∎ ∎	353	peach flesh
w w	407	rose brown, dk.
· ·	437	tan, lt.
◔ ◔	501	blue-green, dk.
n n	502	blue-green
t t	504	blue-green, lt.
L L	564	jade, v. lt.
ı ı	743	yellow, med.
ı ı	745	yellow, lt. pale
\ \	754	peach flesh, lt.
∧ ∧	758	terra cotta, lt.
− −	760	salmon
z z	762	pearl grey, v. lt.
u u	775	baby blue, lt.
∎ ∎	792	cornflower blue, dk.
▲ ▲	793	cornflower blue, med.
s s	819	baby pink, lt.
N N	840	beige-brown, med.
T T	841	beige-brown, lt.
/ /	842	beige-brown, v. lt.
ı ı	948	peach flesh, v. lt.
⊥ ⊥	950	rose brown, lt.
∩ ∩	951	rose brown, v. lt.
∎ ∎	961	dusty rose, dk.
⊚ ⊚	962	dusty rose, med.
D D	963	dusty rose, v. lt.
⅓ ⅓	3046	yellow beige, med.
▸ ▸	3326	rose, lt.
o o	3328	salmon, med.
x x	3685	mauve, dk.
▾ ▾	3687	mauve
⅄ ⅄	3688	mauve, med.
⊙⊙	3689	mauve, lt.
U U	3708	melon, lt.

Backstitch

	208	*bottom border flower beneath girl*
	340	*bottom border flower beneath boy*
	341	*boy's breath*
	792	*lettering, ice, snow at boy's feet*
	839	*boy, girl, branches, bird, nest, grass, flowers*

French knot

·	839	*branch blossoms, bird's eye, butterfly*

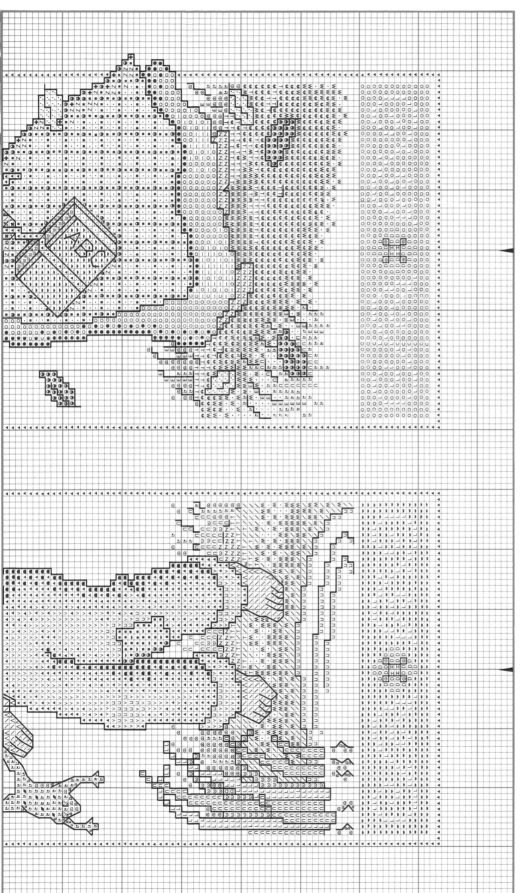

This set of the four seasons can be worked on a single cloth, or on four separate pieces matted with four openings in one frame.

DMC Six-Strand Floss

Cross-stitch

		white
●●	221	shell pink, dk.
℮℮	309	rose, deep
++	318	steel grey, lt.
◑◑	352	coral, lt.
▪▪	353	peach flesh
⅃⅃	368	pistachio green, lt.
◎◎	369	pistachio green, v. lt.
ww	407	rose brown, dk.
·:·	437	tan, lt.
LL	564	jade, v. lt.
EE	677	old gold, v. lt.
MM	712	cream
✗✗	722	orange spice, lt.
ıı	738	tan, v. lt.
ıı	743	yellow, med.
II	745	yellow, lt. pale
88	746	off white
\\\\	754	peach flesh, lt.
∧∧	758	terra cotta, lt.
−−	760	salmon
ZZ	762	pearl grey, v. lt.
∪∪	775	baby blue, lt.
▲▲	792	cornflower blue, dk.
▲▲	793	cornflower blue, med.
∨∨	809	delft
NN	840	beige-brown, med.
TT	841	beige-brown, lt.
∕∕	842	beige-brown, v. lt.
ıı	948	peach flesh, v. lt.
⊥⊥	950	rose brown, lt.
∩∩	951	rose brown, v. lt.
◉◉	962	dusty rose, med.
DD	963	dusty rose, v. lt.
◢◢	992	aquamarine
↳↳	3046	yellow beige, med.
○○	3328	salmon, med.
▮▮	3341	apricot
❤❤	3687	mauve
⊞⊞	3688	mauve, med.
◑◑	3689	mauve, lt.
∪∪	3708	melon, lt.

Backstitch

	white	*ABC on book*
	309	*cherries*
	352	*worm in bird's beak*
	792	*pond water, lettering*
	839	*boy, girl, frog, branches, leaves, grass, birds, nest*
	3328	*bottom border flower beneath girl*
	3687	*bottom border flower beneath boy*

French knot

··	839	*birds' eyes*

LITTLE DROPS OF WATER

Shown on page 34

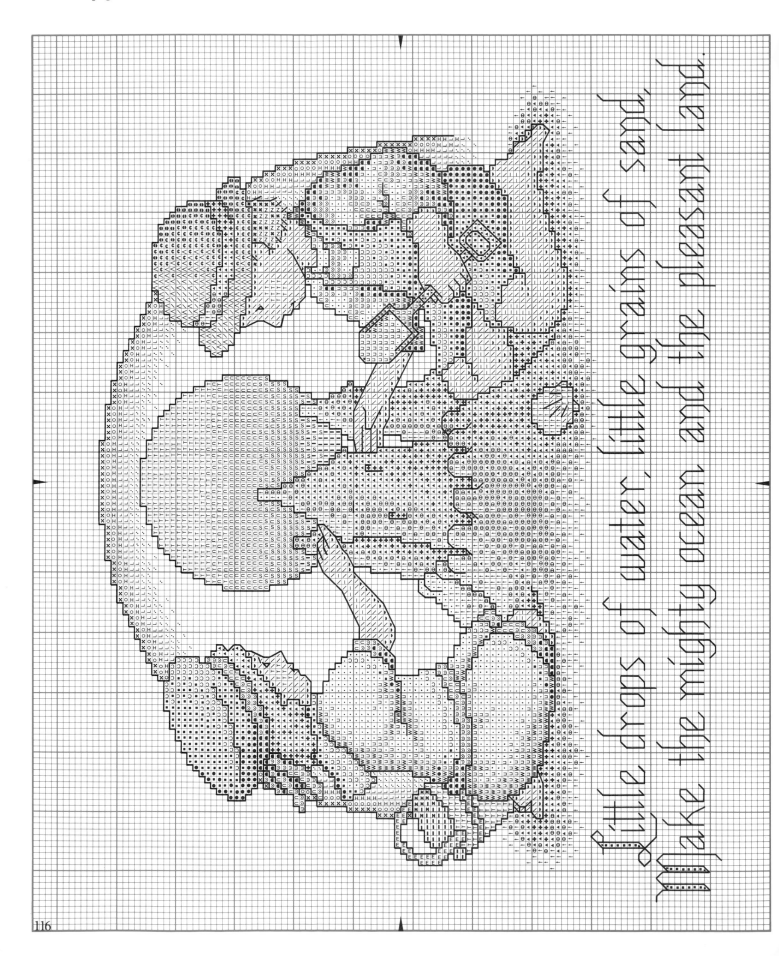

JUNE BRINGS TULIPS

SACHET BAG • Shown on page 1

The original design was worked on aida 14 using 3 strands embroidery floss for cross-stitch and 2 strands for backstitch. Before starting, see *How Many Strands*, page 66.

Fabric	Design size	Fabric size for project shown
Aida 11	13½" × 10"	20" × 16"
Aida 14	10" × 7⅛"	17" × 13"
Aida 18	8¼" × 6"	14" × 12"
Hardanger 22	6¾" × 5"	13" × 11"
Linen 32 (over 2)	9½" × 6¾"	15½" × 13"

DMC Six-Strand Floss

Cross-stitch

· ·		white
† †		ecru
I I	210	lavender, med.
W W	318	steel grey, lt.
ʊ ʊ	335	rose
ᴑ ᴑ	341	blue violet, lt.
− −	352	coral, lt.
T T	353	peach flesh
✦ ✦	407	rose brown, dk.
✻ ✻	435	brown, v. lt.
N N	437	tan, lt.
ᴑ ᴑ	543	beige-brown, ultra lt.
⹀ ⹀	645	beaver grey, v. dk.
X X	742	tangerine, lt.
o o	743	yellow, med.
I I	744	yellow, pale
L L	745	yellow, lt. pale
·.·	746	off white
\ \	754	peach flesh, lt.
⌐ ⌐	758	terra cotta, lt.
ᴜ ᴜ	762	pearl grey, v. lt.
∩ ∩	776	pink, med.
● ●	792	cornflower blue, dk.
■ ■	793	cornflower blue, med.
− −	948	peach flesh, v. lt.
▲ ▲	950	rose brown, lt.
ᴖ ᴖ	3022	brown-grey, med.
ʌ ʌ	3023	brown-grey, lt.
∕ ∕	3033	mocha brown, v. lt.
⫶ ⫶	3328	salmon, med.
▪ ▪	3350	dusty rose, v. dk.
m m	3608	plum, v. lt.
ᴕ ᴕ	3609	plum, ultra lt.

Backstitch

⌐	838	*children, castle, bucket, lettering*
⌐	841	*sun*
⌐	3328	*yellow arch*

French knot

·	838	*punctuation*

Create a personalized sachet bag using the June bouquet of flowers. Use alphabets 7 and 9, pages 156 and 157, for initials. Use light violet (DMC 554) for the small initials and light melon (DMC 3708) with light violet for the large initial.

The sachet bag was worked on aida 14 using 2 strands embroidery floss for cross-stitch and 1 strand for backstitch.

Fabric	Design size	Fabric size for project shown
Aida 14	4¼" × 3½"	10" × 10"
Linen 32 (over 2)	3¾" × 3⅛"	10" × 10"

DMC Six-Strand Floss

Cross-stitch

▲ ▲	335	rose
ᴑ ᴑ	353	peach flesh
✦ ✦	407	rose brown, dk.
ᴕ ᴕ	554	violet, lt.
7 7	818	baby pink
● ●	826	blue, med.
P P	954	nile green
ᴖ ᴖ	992	aquamarine
m m	3708	melon, lt.

Backstitch

⌐	902	*all*

French knot

·	902	*butterfly*

Shown on page 35

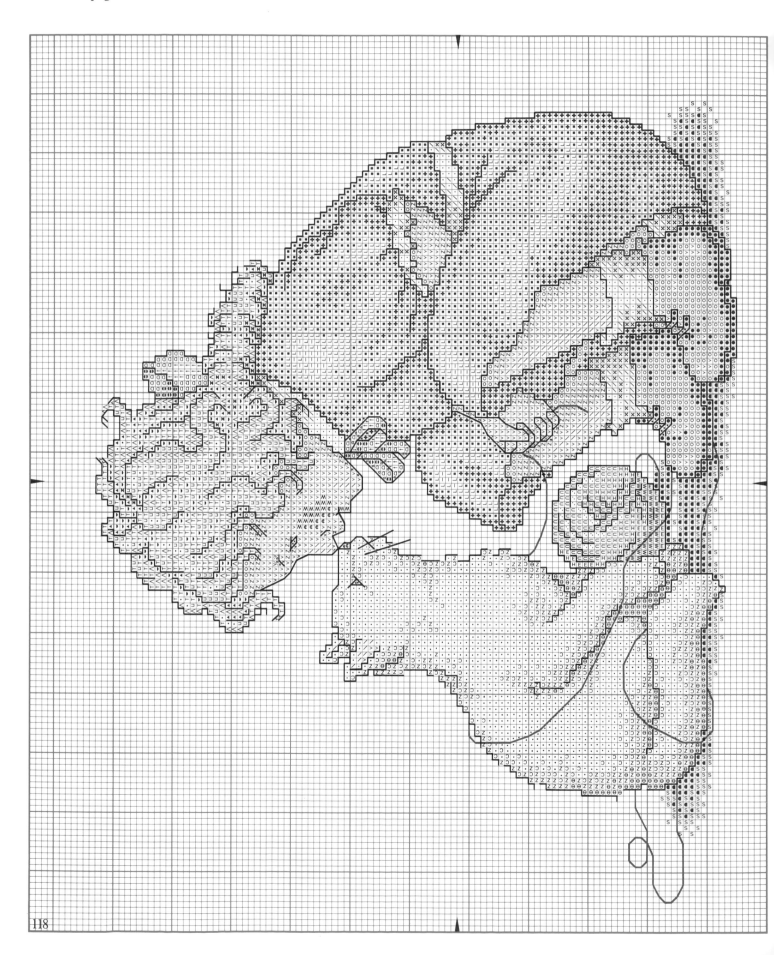

HOT JULY

FRUIT BASKET ❧ Shown on page 1

When embroidering hands and faces, in order to create greater realism and expression, the backstitch line does not always run from corner to corner in the grid. Follow the chart carefully.

The original design was worked on aida 14 using 3 strands embroidery floss for cross-stitch and 2 strands (or 3 strands as noted) for backstitch. Before starting, see *How Many Strands,* page 66.

Fabric	Design size	Fabric size for project shown
Aida 11	11¾″ × 10″	18″ × 16″
Aida 14	9¼″ × 7⅛″	15″ × 13″
Aida 18	7⅛″ × 6″	13″ × 12″
Hardanger 22	5⅞″ × 5″	12″ × 11″
Linen 32 (over 2)	8″ × 6¾″	14″ × 13″

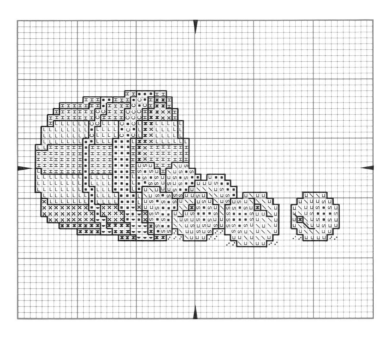

The fruit basket, pictured in the hoop and appearing on page 34, was worked on aida 14 using 3 strands embroidery floss for cross-stitch and 2 strands for backstitch. Before starting, see *How Many Strands,* page 66.

DMC Six-Strand Floss

Cross-stitch

· ·		white
u u		ecru
+ +	311	navy blue, med.
▪ ▪	334	baby blue, med.
m m	351	coral
I I	352	coral, lt.
3 3	353	peach flesh
M M	356	terra cotta, med.
N N	543	beige-brown, ultra lt.
● ●	632	rose brown, v. dk.
◼ ◼	645	beaver grey, v. dk.
∧ ∧	676	old gold, lt.
T T	677	old gold, v. lt.
- -	729	old gold, med.
u u	746	off white
v v	754	peach flesh, lt.
z z	758	terra cotta, lt.
∩ ∩	760	salmon
- -	775	baby blue, lt.
⊕ ⊕	842	beige-brown, v. lt.
✗ ✗	869	hazel nut brown, v. dk.
∽ ∽	927	grey-green, med.
\ \	948	peach flesh, v. lt.
·. ·.	951	rose brown, v. lt.
◻ ◻	962	dusty rose, med.
× ×	3022	brown-grey, med.
╱ ╱	3024	brown-grey, v. lt.
▲ ▲	3045	yellow beige, dk.
○ ○	3064	rose brown, med.
L L	3325	baby blue
∩ ∩	3341	apricot
⊝ ⊝	3350	dusty rose, v. dk.
┼ ┼	3689	mauve, lt.

Backstitch

⌐	351	*strand of yarn (3 strands)*
⌐	838	*all other backstitch*

DMC Six-Strand Floss

Cross-stitch

▪ ▪	335	rose
∽ ∽	352	coral, lt.
u u	353	peach flesh
✗ ✗	407	rose brown
\ \	745	yellow, lt. pale
○ ○	776	pink, med.
L L	945	rose brown
× ×	950	rose brown, lt.
I I	951	rose brown, v. lt.
·. ·.	3033	mocha brown, v. lt.
- -	3350	dusty rose, v. dk.

Backstitch

⌐	838	*all*

JACK AND JILL

Shown on page 37

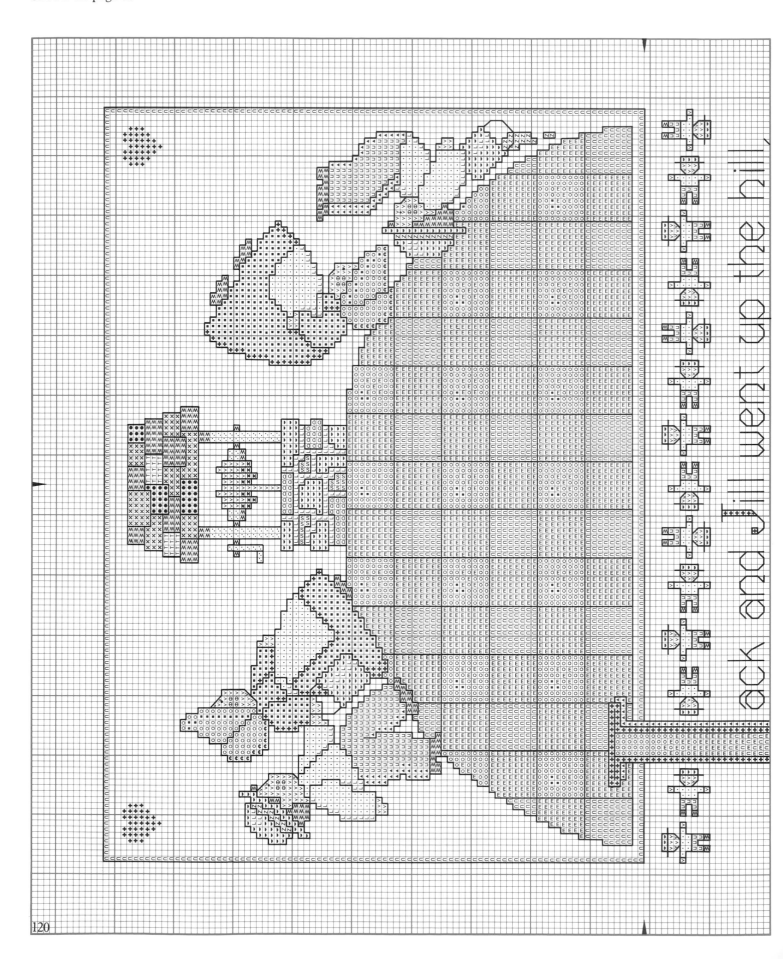

Jack and Jill are mentioned occasionally in the works of Shakespeare though he was probably not referring to the rhyme. In his day "Jack" and "Jill" were synonyms for "lad" and "lass."

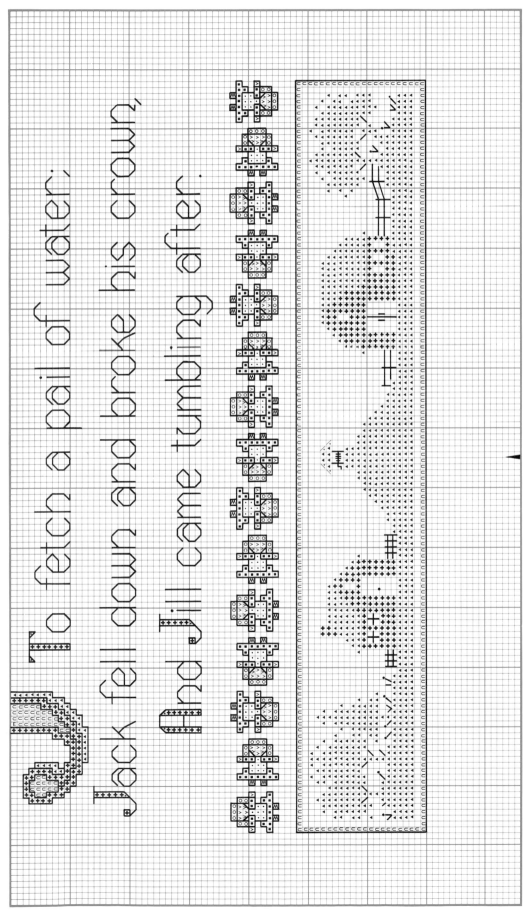

For a smaller project, eliminate the farm silhouette.

When working large areas, such as the farm silhouette, purchase all embroidery floss from the same dye-lot. To minimize flecks of fabric showing through, pull stitches uniformly taut, but not too tight.

The original design was worked on aida 14 using 3 strands embroidery floss for cross-stitch and 2 strands (or 1 strand as noted) for backstitch. Before starting, see *How Many Strands*, page 66.

Fabric	Design size	Fabric size for project shown
Aida 11	11¾″ × 16¾″	18″ × 23″
Aida 14	9¼″ × 13¼″	15″ × 19″
Aida 18	7¼″ × 10¼″	13″ × 16½″
Hardanger 22	5⅞″ × 8½″	12″ × 14½″
Linen 32 (over 2)	8⅛″ × 11½″	14″ × 18″

DMC Six-Strand Floss

Cross-stitch

··		white
--	318	steel grey, lt.
TT	352	coral, lt.
ΦΦ	353	peach flesh
××	356	terra cotta, med.
LL	415	pearl grey
∩∩	676	old gold, lt.
oo	745	yellow, lt. pale
vv	754	peach flesh, lt.
xx	758	terra cotta, lt.
••	760	salmon
nn	827	blue, v. lt.
zz	828	blue, ultra lt.
□□	927	grey-green, med.
▲▲	930	antique blue, dk.
uu	931	antique blue, med.
··	950	rose brown, lt.
mm	955	nile green, lt.
++	962	dusty rose, med.
ss	3042	antique violet, lt.
⋗⋗	3064	rose brown, med.
∎∎	3326	rose, lt.

Backstitch

	930	*tumbling tot border designs (1 strand)*
	930	*all but plaid hill*
	3326	*lines in hill*

French knot

·	930	*children's eyes, punctuation, doorknob*
·	962	*flowers in silhouette landscape*

THERE WAS ONCE A FISH

Shown on page 36

Here is an enthusiastic tribute to the fisherman in your house. The little girl's expression says gently and without words, "You caught it. You clean it!"

When embroidering hands and faces, in order to create greater realism and expression, the backstitch line does not always run from corner to corner in the grid. Follow the chart carefully.

The original design was worked on aida 14 using 3 strands embroidery floss for cross-stitch and 2 strands for backstitch. Before starting, see *How Many Strands*, page 66.

Fabric	Design size	Fabric size for project shown
Aida 11	11⅜″ × 6⅞″	18″ × 13″
Aida 14	9″ × 5⅜″	15″ × 12″
Aida 18	7″ × 4¼″	13″ × 10″
Hardanger 22	5⅝″ × 3⅜″	12″ × 9″
Linen 32 (over 2)	7¾″ × 4¾″	14″ × 11″

DMC Six-Strand Floss

		Cross-stitch
· ·		white
╱ ╱	322	navy blue, v. lt.
+ +	353	peach flesh
Φ Φ	407	rose brown, dk.
T T	422	hazel nut brown, lt.
ᴄ ᴄ	437	tan, lt.
⊕ ⊕	500	blue-green, v. dk.
◖ ◗	501	blue-green, dk.
ı ı	503	blue-green, med.
⌐ ⌐	504	blue-green, lt.
⊤ ⊤	543	beige-brown, ultra lt.
● ●	563	jade, lt.
◀ ◀	645	beaver grey, v. dk.
m m	676	old gold, lt.
E E	712	cream
n n	738	tan, v. lt.
∧ ∧	739	tan, ultra lt.
ம ம	744	yellow, pale
v v	745	yellow, lt. pale
ᴖ ᴖ	746	off white
╲ ╲	754	peach flesh, lt.
ᵛ ᵛ	758	terra cotta, lt.
◉ ◉	760	salmon
ɪ ɪ	775	baby blue, lt.
▲ ▲	813	blue, lt.
⠒⠒	818	baby pink
o o	827	blue, v. lt.
■ ■	839	beige-brown, dk.
× ×	840	beige-brown, med.
Λ Λ	841	beige-brown, lt.
ʟ ʟ	842	beige-brown, v. lt.
u u	948	peach flesh, v. lt.
╳ ╳	955	nile green, lt.
ᴢ ᴢ	961	dusty rose, dk.
z z	3022	brown-grey, med.
ᴑ ᴑ	3023	brown-grey, lt.
w w	3033	mocha brown, v. lt.
◓ ◓	3326	rose, lt.
ᵡ ᵡ	3328	salmon, med.
		Backstitch
	838	*all*

ALL WORK AND NO PLAY

Shown on page 38

The original design was worked on aida 14 using 3 strands embroidery floss for cross-stitch and 2 strands for backstitch. Before starting, see *How Many Strands*, page 66.

Fabric	Design size	Fabric size for project shown
Aida 11	11⅞″ × 8¼″	18″ × 14″
Aida 14	9¼″ × 6½″	15″ × 12½″
Aida 18	7⅛″ × 5″	13″ × 11″
Hardanger 22	5⅞″ × 4⅛″	12″ × 10″
Linen 32 (over 2)	8⅛″ × 5⅝″	14″ × 12″

DMC Six-Strand Floss

Cross-stitch

··		white
▾▾	309	rose, deep
××	318	steel grey, lt.
▲▲	347	salmon, dk.
▪▪	352	coral, lt.
ıı	353	peach flesh
∩∩	368	pistachio green, lt.
⊙⊙	543	beige-brown, ultra lt.
✗✗	632	rose brown, v. dk.
≢≢	743	yellow, mcd.
ww	744	yellow, pale
--	745	yellow, lt. pale
\\	754	peach flesh, lt.
▫▫	758	terra cotta, lt.
∨∨	760	salmon
◦◦	762	pearl grey, v. lt.
∧∧	775	baby blue, lt.
●●	798	delft, dk.
mm	799	delft, med.
⊤⊤	800	delft, pale
▲▲	840	beige-brown, med.
ꞯꞯ	841	beige-brown, lt.
⊕⊕	842	beige-brown, v. lt.
HH	899	rose, med.
·.·.	948	peach flesh, v. lt.
ss	950	rose brown, lt.
LL	951	rose brown, v. lt.
✦✦	987	forest green, dk.
zz	989	forest green
oo	3064	rose brown, med.
⊞⊞	3328	salmon, med.

Backstitch

	838	*boy, corn, basket, lettering*
	3064	*corn silk*

French knot

·	838	*punctuation*

IF YOU ARE TO BE A GENTLEMAN

Shown on page 39

Many tickling games claim to foretell the future. For example, when children are tickled in the palm of the hand, the first thing they say will be the first thing they say after being married.

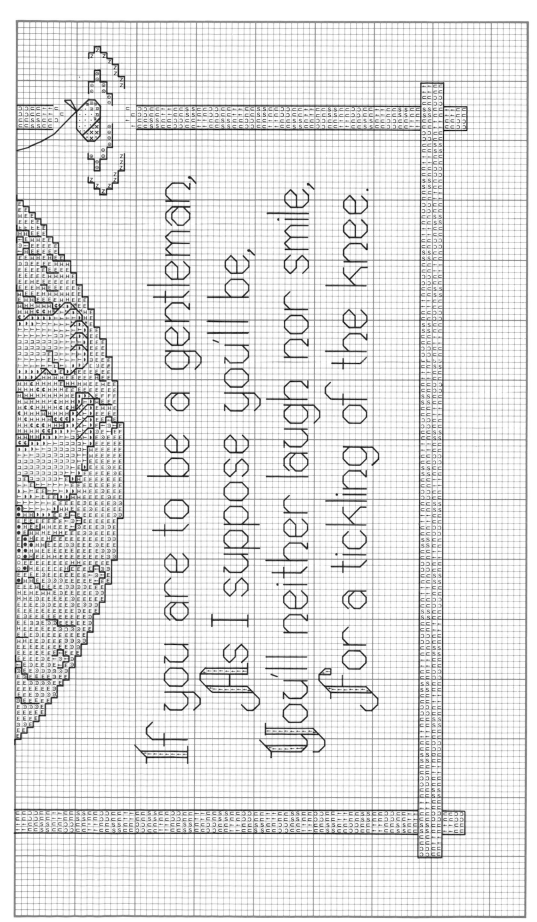

When embroidering hands and faces, in order to create greater realism and expression, the backstitch line does not always run from corner to corner in the grid. Follow the chart carefully.

The original design was worked on aida 14 using 3 strands embroidery floss for cross-stitch and 2 strands for backstitch. Before starting, see *How Many Strands*, page 66.

Fabric	Design size	Fabric size for project shown
Aida 11	12¼″ × 17¼″	18″ × 23″
Aida 14	9¾″ × 13½″	16″ × 19½″
Aida 18	7½″ × 10½″	13½″ × 16½″
Hardanger 22	6¼″ × 8⅝″	12″ × 14½″
Linen 32 (over 2)	8½″ × 11⅞″	14½″ × 18″

DMC Six-Strand Floss

Cross-stitch

· ·		white
ɩ ɩ	210	lavender, med.
⊥ ⊥	320	pistachio green, med.
o o	322	navy blue, v. lt.
⊙ ⊙	334	baby blue, med.
8 8	353	peach flesh
x x	407	rose brown, dk.
ɪ ɪ	414	steel grey, dk.
ʋ ʋ	415	pearl grey
● ●	435	brown, v. lt.
■ ■	437	tan, lt.
z z	561	jade, v. dk.
∴ ∴	712	cream
∧ ∧	738	tan, v. lt.
⊚ ⊚	745	yellow, lt. pale
т т	754	peach flesh, lt.
▬ ▬	758	terra cotta, lt.
╱ ╱	775	baby blue, lt.
◡ ◡	776	pink, med.
n n	839	beige-brown, dk.
▲ ▲	840	beige-brown, med.
Φ Φ	841	beige-brown, lt.
L L	842	beige-brown, v. lt.
✕ ✕	899	rose, med.
●● ●●	930	antique blue, dk.
u u	948	peach flesh, v. lt.
◌ ◌	966	baby green, med.
◓ ◓	991	aquamarine, dk.
N N	3325	baby blue
m m	3348	yellow green, lt.
s s	3609	plum, ultra lt.

Backstitch

⌐	839	*all*

French knot

·	838	*punctuation, butterfly*

Sleep, Baby, Sleep

Shown on page 41

Sheep and other animals are often summoned at bedtime. Once it was believed they stood a little nearer to "paradise."

You might wish to abbreviate the design by working only the lower portion enclosing the verse. To do this, extend the red outer border across the top of the verse; work two spaces above the tree leaves hanging over the words.

When working large areas, such as silhouettes, purchase all embroidery floss from the same dye-lot. To minimize flecks of fabric showing through, pull stitches uniformly taut, but not too tight.

The original design was worked on aida 14 using 3 strands embroidery floss for cross-stitch and 2 strands for backstitch. Before starting, see *How Many Strands,* page 66.

Fabric	Design size	Fabric size for project shown
Aida 11	13¾″ × 18½″	20″ × 25″
Aida 14	10¾″ × 14⅞″	17″ × 21″
Aida 18	8¾″ × 12″	14½″ × 18″
Hardanger 22	6⅞″ × 9½″	13″ × 15½″
Linen 32 (over 2)	9⅜″ × 12⅞″	15½″ × 19″

DMC Six-Strand Floss

Cross-stitch

	353	peach flesh
	712	cream
	754	peach flesh, lt.
	760	salmon
	930	antique blue, dk.
	951	rose brown, v. lt.
	3350	dusty rose, v. dk.

Backstitch

	930	*lettering, butterfly, cradle strings*

French knot

	930	*punctuation*

127

MARY HAD A LITTLE LAMB

Shown on page 43

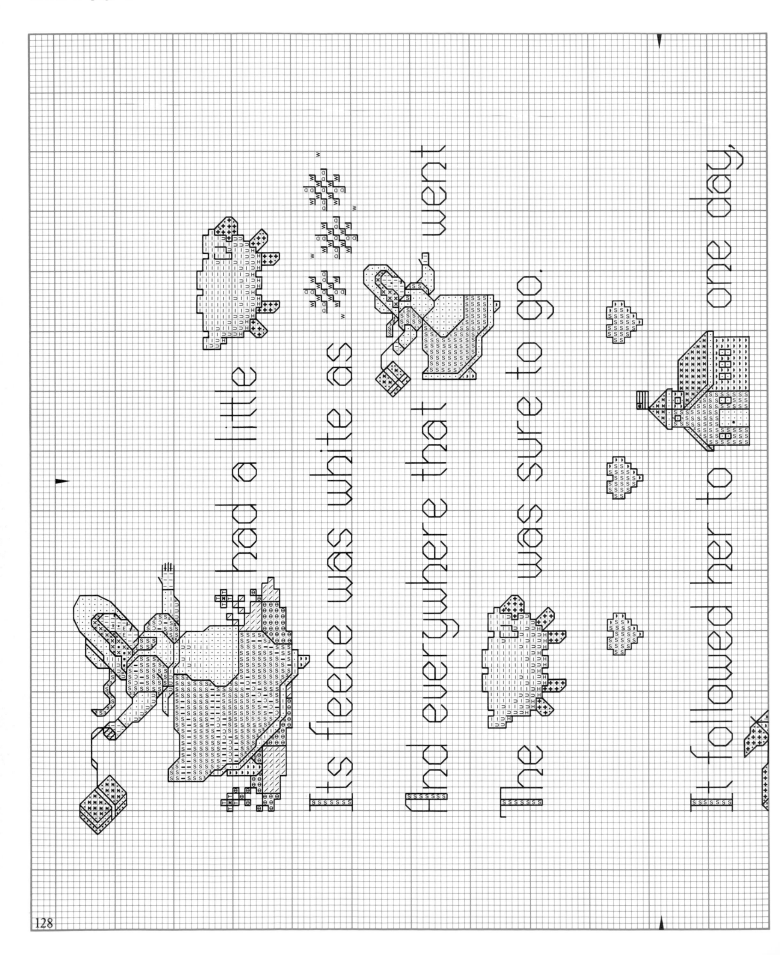

Mary Sawyer, an eleven-year-old schoolgirl who once had a lamb, always gave full credit to twelve-year-old John Roulstone for writing and giving to her what were to become the most familiar verses in American literature. The poem was first printed in 1830. Thomas Edison recited the lines in 1877, making them the first words ever recorded and reproduced on his phonograph.

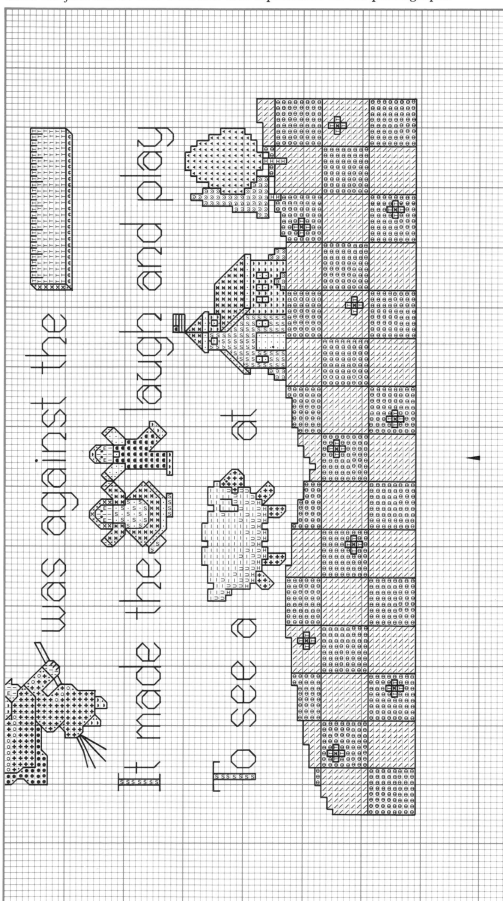

A rebus, combining words and pictures, is always a favorite with children. The first two verses of "Mary Had a Little Lamb" make a delightful rebus sampler, but the first verse can stand alone if a smaller project is desired.

The original design was worked on aida 14 using 3 strands embroidery floss for cross-stitch and 2 strands (or 1 as noted) for backstitch. Before starting, see *How Many Strands*, page 66.

Fabric	Design size	Fabric size for project shown
Aida 11	10⅞″ × 16¾″	17″ × 23″
Aida 14	8⅝″ × 13¼″	15″ × 19″
Aida 18	6⅝″ × 10¼″	13″ × 16½″
Hardanger 22	5½″ × 8½″	11½″ × 14½″
Linen 32 (over 2)	7½″ × 11½″	14″ × 18″

DMC Six-Strand Floss

Cross-stitch

. .		white
- -		ecru
● ●	322	navy blue, v. lt.
m m	353	peach flesh
∩ ∩	402	mahogany, v. lt.
+ +	451	shell grey, dk.
I I	453	shell grey, lt.
▲ ▲	562	jade, med.
\ \	564	jade, v. lt.
■ ■	743	yellow, med.
T T	744	yellow, pale
x x	745	yellow, lt. pale
I I	754	peach flesh, lt.
o o	762	pearl grey, v. lt.
◡ ◡	776	pink, med.
w w	799	delft, med.
□ □	800	delft, pale
● ●	931	antique blue, med.
⊙ ⊙	991	aquamarine, dk.
Φ Φ	992	aquamarine
U U	3033	mocha brown, v. lt.
▬ ▬	3328	salmon, med.
x x	3341	apricot
s s	3706	melon, med.
I I	3708	melon, lt.

Backstitch

	902	*lettering, art except flag stripes*
	3706	*flag stripes (1 strand)*

French knot

•	902	*punctuation, eyes, doorknobs*

A NEAT LITTLE CLOCK

Shown on page 42

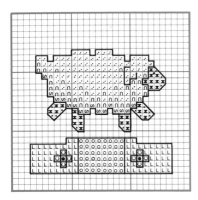

The lamb appearing in the what-not shelf was worked on aida 14 using 2 strands embroidery floss for cross-stitch and 1 strand for backstitch.

Fabric	Design size	Fabric size for project shown
Aida 14	2″ × 2″	8″ × 8″

DMC Six-Strand Floss

Cross-stitch

∴∴		ecru
✗✗	451	shell grey, dk.
ss	453	shell grey, lt.
LL	564	jade, v. lt.
∪∪	744	yellow, pale
oo	992	aquamarine
nn	3033	mocha brown, v. lt.
●●	3341	apricot

Backstitch

	902	*all*

French knot

•	902	*lamb's eye*

The original design was worked on aida 14 using 3 strands embroidery floss for cross-stitch and 2 strands for backstitch. Before starting, see *How Many Strands*, page 66.

When finished, consider framing this country school scene with a slate board (see page 64). Then you can either chalk up reminders to your young scholars or give the project as a special gift to a favorite teacher.

Fabric	Design size	Fabric size for project shown
Aida 11	9″ × 9″	15″ × 15″
Aida 14	7″ × 7″	13″ × 13″
Aida 18	5½″ × 5½″	11″ × 11″
Hardanger 22	4½″ × 4½″	10½″ × 10½″
Linen 32 (over 2)	6¼″ × 6¼″	12″ × 12″

DMC Six-Strand Floss

Cross-stitch

		white
ЯЯ	209	lavender, dk.
↑↑	210	lavender, med.
∴∴	211	lavender, lt.
✗✗	335	rose
↘↘	347	salmon, dk.
●●	351	coral
◖◗	352	coral, lt.
⊜⊜	353	peach flesh
mm	407	rose brown, dk.
▲▲	420	hazel nut brown, dk.
ıı	422	hazel nut brown, lt.
⋈⋈	436	tan
⊤⊤	437	tan, lt.
oo	543	beige-brown, ultra lt.
ıııı	632	rose brown, v. dk.
⊍⊍	676	old gold, lt.
LL	712	cream
∩∩	744	yellow, pale
oo	745	yellow, lt. pale
⊥⊥	746	off white
\\	754	peach flesh, lt.
uu	758	terra cotta, lt.
✦✦	792	cornflower blue, dk.
▲▲	793	cornflower blue, med.
vv	794	cornflower blue, lt.
∧∧	800	delft, pale
▲▲	801	coffee brown, dk.
▾▾	809	delft
●●	839	beige-brown, dk.
✗✗	840	beige-brown, med.
✕✕	841	beige-brown, lt.
ss	842	beige-brown, v. lt.
ww	869	hazel nut brown, v. dk.
−−	948	peach flesh, v. lt.
⊥⊥	950	rose brown, lt.
▪▪	962	dusty rose, med.
⊙⊙	989	forest green
cc	3348	yellow-green, lt.
⊕⊕	3705	melon, dk.

Backstitch

	355	*children's books*
	809	*vertical lines in apron plaid*
	838	*children, bench, books on bench, apple*
	840	*clock*
	962	*horizontal lines in apron plaid*

French knot

•	838	*shoes*
•	840	*clock face*

Books were scarce in colonial days. Children often wrote protective verses inside their schoolbooks. Some were simple, "Steal not this book for fear or shame: For here you read the owner's name." Some were quite graphic, "Steal not this book my honest friend/For fear the gallos will be your end/The gallos is high, the rope is strong,/To steal this book you know is wrong."

End of bench

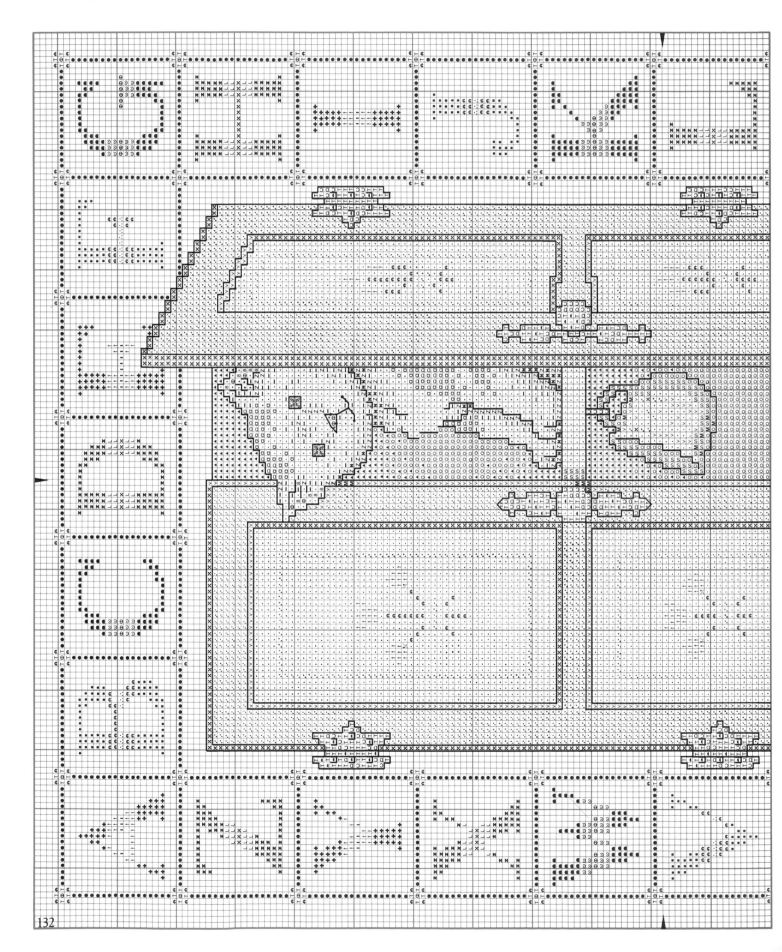

Of all the motifs associated with the traditional schoolgirl sampler, the alphabet is first and foremost. However, throughout the 18th century many young students of the needle crafts endured the stitching of complete multiplication tables, almanacs, world maps, and large public buildings.

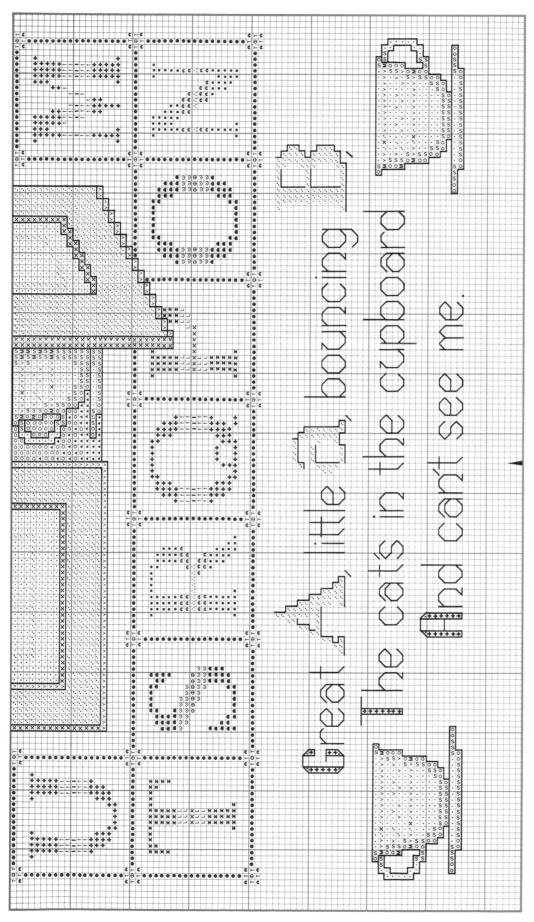

The original design was worked on aida 14 using 3 strands embroidery floss for cross-stitch and 2 strands for backstitch. Before starting, see *How Many Strands*, page 66.

Fabric	Design size	Fabric size for project shown
Aida 11	13¾″ × 18″	20″ × 24″
Aida 14	10¾″ × 14⅜″	17″ × 20″
Aida 18	8⅜″ × 11″	14½″ × 17″
Hardanger 22	6⅞″ × 9⅛″	13″ × 15″
Linen 32 (over 2)	9⅜″ × 12½″	15½″ × 18″

DMC Six-Strand Floss

Cross-stitch

Symbol	No.	Color
··		white
– –		ecru
M M	312	navy blue, lt.
▲ ▲	317	pewter grey
o o	318	steel grey, lt.
v v	334	baby blue, med.
x x	340	blue violet, med.
L L	341	blue violet, lt.
s s	415	pearl grey
Z Z	543	beige-brown, ultra lt.
∴∴	564	jade, v. lt.
ʊ ʊ	676	old gold, lt.
T T	744	yellow, pale
▲ ▲	746	off white
8 8	754	peach flesh, lt.
ʊ ʊ	760	salmon
Φ Φ	761	salmon, lt.
x x	775	baby blue, lt.
w w	839	beige-brown, dk.
H H	842	beige-brown, v. lt.
●●	930	antique blue, dk.
ʊ ʊ	945	rose brown
∎ ∎	992	aquamarine
∩ ∩	993	aquamarine, lt.
▢ ▢	3064	rose brown, med.
··	3325	baby blue
▲ ▲	3328	salmon, med.
+ +	3687	mauve
↑ ↑	3688	mauve, med.
l l	3689	mauve, lt.

Backstitch

	No.	
⌐⌐	839	*cat, cupboard, cups, lettering*
⌐⌐	930	*great A, little a, great B*

French knot

	No.	
·	839	*cat's nose and mouth, punctuation*

133

I Had a Little Hobby Horse

Shown on page 44

I had a little hobby horse
And it was dapple gray,
Its head was made of pea-straw,
Its tail was made of hay.

SEPTEMBER OFFERS

CORNUCOPIA ❧ Shown on page 42

When embroidering hands and faces, in order to create greater realism and expression, the backstitch line does not always run from corner to corner in the grid. Follow the chart carefully.

The original design was worked on aida 14 using 3 strands embroidery floss for cross-stitch and 2 strands for backstitch. Before starting, see *How Many Strands*, page 66.

Fabric	Design size	Fabric size for project shown
Aida 11	11″ × 12¾″	17″ × 19″
Aida 14	8½″ × 10″	14½″ × 16″
Aida 18	6⅝″ × 7¾″	13″ × 14″
Hardanger 22	5½″ × 6⅜″	11½″ × 12½″
Linen 32 (over 2)	7½″ × 8¾″	13½″ × 15″

DMC Six-Strand Floss

Cross-stitch

· ·		white
⊠ ⊠	221	shell pink, dk.
∩ ∩	223	shell pink, med.
I I	224	shell pink, lt.
─ ─	225	shell pink, v. lt.
R R	318	steel grey, lt.
M M	350	coral, med.
u u	352	coral, lt.
X X	353	peach flesh
v v	407	rose brown, dk.
= =	632	rose brown, v. dk.
m m	676	old gold, lt.
▲ ▲	712	cream
● ●	738	tan, v. lt.
○ ○	745	yellow, lt. pale
A A	746	off white
\ \	754	peach flesh, lt.
c c	758	terra cotta, lt.
L L	762	pearl grey, v. lt.
e e	775	baby blue, lt.
G G	899	rose, med.
▣ ▣	930	antique blue, dk.
⊕ ⊕	931	antique blue, med.
⸬ ⸬	932	antique blue, lt.
I I	948	peach flesh, v. lt.
N N	950	rose brown, lt.
⋔ ⋔	991	aquamarine, dk.
⌐ ⌐	992	aquamarine
■ ■	3024	brown grey, v. lt.

Backstitch

	839	*boy, horse, lettering*
	930	*borders, floor moulding, silhouette horses*

French knot

·	839	*punctuation*

The original design was worked on aida 14 using 3 strands embroidery floss for cross-stitch and 2 strands for backstitch. Before starting, see *How Many Strands*, page 66.

Fabric	Design size	Fabric size for project shown
Aida 11	5½″ × 4½″	12½″ × 10½″
Aida 14	4¼″ × 3⅝″	10″ × 10″
Linen 32 (over 2)	3¾″ × 3⅛″	10″ × 10″

DMC Six-Strand Floss

Cross-stitch

● ●	347	salmon, dk.
N N	351	coral
▾ ▾	352	coral, lt.
○ ○	420	hazel nut brown, dk.
4 4	422	hazel nut brown, lt.
X X	676	old gold, lt.
▲ ▲	680	old gold, dk.
⋅ ⋅	712	cream
A A	744	yellow, pale
○ ○	745	yellow, lt. pale
T T	746	off white
- -	754	peach flesh, lt.
e e	760	salmon
▲ ▲	801	coffee brown, dk.
⊠ ⊠	869	hazel nut brown, v. dk.
\ \	989	forest green
v v	3348	yellow-green, lt.
P P	3685	mauve, dk.
I I	3688	mauve, med.
○ ○	3705	melon, dk.

Backstitch

	838	*cornucopia, fruit, lettering*
	3345	*vine, leaves*

THREE LITTLE GHOSTESSES

Shown on page 47

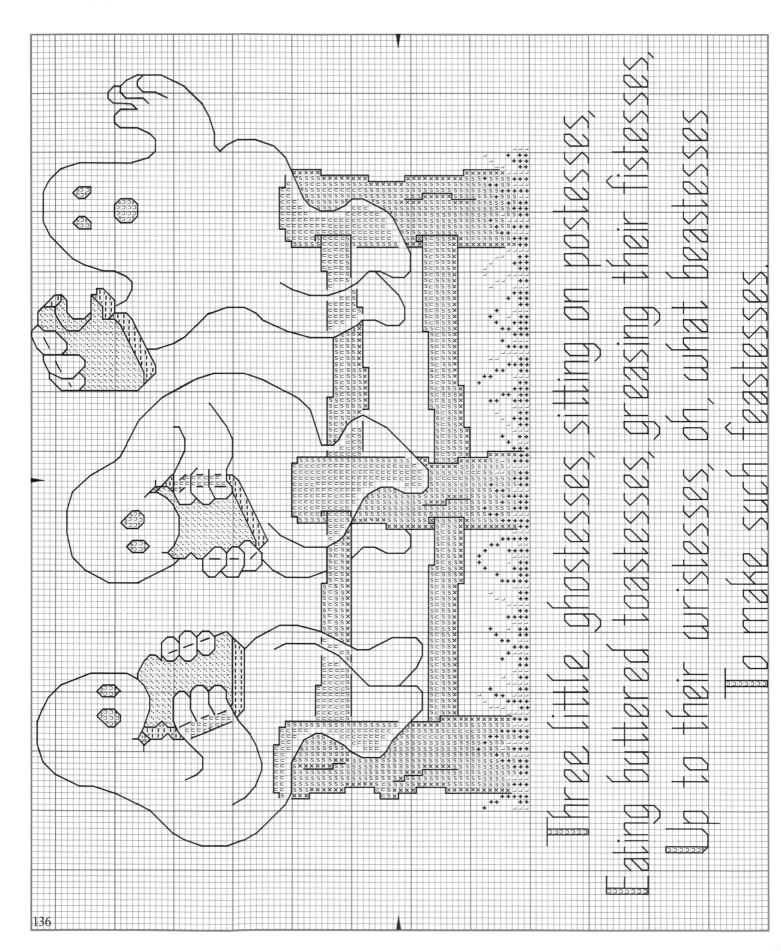

Three little ghostesses, sitting on postesses,

Eating buttered toastesses, greasing their fistesses,

Up to their wristesses, oh what beastesses,

To make such feastesses.

GIRL'S ROOM SIGN ⌐ Shown on page 1

The original design was worked on aida 14 using 3 strands embroidery floss for cross-stitch and 2 strands for backstitch.

Fabric	Design size	Fabric size for project shown
Aida 11	13½″ × 11¼″	19½″ × 17″
Aida 14	10¾″ × 8½″	17″ × 14½″
Linen 32 (over 2)	9½″ × 7¾″	15″ × 14″

Cross-stitch

--	402	mahogany, v. lt.
oo	415	pearl grey
××	435	brown, v. lt.
ss	437	tan, lt.
++	562	jade, med.
··	712	cream
nn	951	rose brown, v. lt.
LL	989	forest green

Backstitch

414	*ghosts*
839	*fence, toast, lettering*
841	*fence, toast inside ghosts*

French knot

•	839	*punctuation*

Designed to complement the Wee Willie Winkie room sign (page 141), this little sleepyhead will make the bedroom a special place for your special girl. Refer to alphabets 6 and 8 on page 156, with the larger alphabet for the first letter of the name. Use dark dusty rose (DMC 961) to cross-stitch the name, and very dark beige-brown (DMC 838) to backstitch.

The original design was worked on aida 14 using 2 strands embroidery floss for cross-stitch and 1 strand for backstitch.

Fabric	Design size	Fabric size for project shown
Aida 14	6½″ × 8½″	12½″ × 14½″

DMC Six-Strand Floss

Cross-stitch

··		white
⊕⊕	317	pewter grey
ѡѡ	318	steel grey, lt.

nn	353	peach flesh
••	368	pistachio green, lt.
mm	407	rose brown, dk.
xx	676	old gold, lt.
ss	712	cream
zz	722	orange spice, lt.
××	744	yellow, pale
//	745	yellow, lt. pale
vv	754	peach flesh, lt.
ʌʌ	758	terra cotta, lt.
--	762	pearl grey, v. lt.
uu	818	baby pink
II	827	blue, v. lt.
····	948	peach flesh, v. lt.
LL	950	rose brown, lt.
TT	951	rose brown, v. lt.
II	955	nile green, lt.
••	961	dusty rose, dk.
TT	3326	rose, lt.

Backstitch

838	*all*

French knot

838	*girl's and doll's eyes*

GOOD NIGHT, SLEEP TIGHT

Shown on page 49

When embroidering hands and faces, in order to create greater realism and expression, the backstitch line does not always run from corner to corner in the grid. Follow the chart carefully.

When working large areas, purchase all embroidery floss from the same dye-lot. To minimize flecks of fabric showing through, pull stitches uniformly taut, but not too tight.

The original design was worked on aida 14 using 3 strands embroidery floss for cross-stitch, 2 strands for backstitch, and 2 strands for satin stitch. Before starting, see *How Many Strands*, page 66.

Fabric	Design size	Fabric size for project shown
Aida 11	10⅞″ × 16¼″	17″ × 22″
Aida 14	8⅝″ × 12⅞″	15″ × 20″
Aida 18	6⅝″ × 10″	13″ × 16″
Hardanger 22	5½″ × 8¼″	11½″ × 15″
Linen 32 (over 2)	7½″ × 11¼″	14″ × 18″

DMC Six-Strand Floss

Cross-stitch

· ·		white
K K	210	lavender, med.
R R	211	lavender, lt.
u u	223	shell pink, med.
A A	224	shell pink, lt.
● ●	312	navy blue, lt.
⌇ ⌇	316	antique mauve, med.
5 5	320	pistachio green, med.
x x	322	navy blue, v. lt.
φ φ	334	baby blue, med.
B B	340	blue violet, med.
w w	353	peach flesh
o o	368	pistachio green, lt.
I I	402	mahogany, v. lt.
◹ ◹	422	hazel nut brown, lt.
H H	437	tan, lt.
8 8	472	avocado green, ultra lt.
҂ ҂	501	blue-green, dk.
m m	502	blue-green
↑ ↑	503	blue-green, med.
φ φ	535	ash grey, v. lt.
⊤ ⊤	543	beige-brown, ultra lt.
— —	554	violet, lt.
P P	677	old gold, v. lt.
↓ ↓	712	cream
ʌ ʌ	739	tan, ultra lt.
4 4	744	yellow, pale
N N	754	peach flesh, lt.
ʊ ʊ	758	terra cotta, lt.
╌ ╌	760	salmon
◡ ◡	761	salmon, lt.
n n	775	baby blue, lt.
v v	776	pink, med.
∟ ∟	800	delft, pale
z z	818	baby pink
✦ ✦	840	beige-brown, med.
N N	841	beige-brown, lt.
I I	842	beige-brown, v. lt.
■ ■	930	antique blue, dk.
⊙ ⊙	931	antique blue, med.
x x	932	antique blue, lt.
Y Y	945	rose brown
∴ ∴	948	peach flesh, v. lt.
G G	962	dusty rose, med.
2 2	966	baby green, med.
҂ ҂	3041	antique violet, med.
▲ ▲	3064	rose brown, med.
ʊ ʊ	3078	golden yellow, v. lt.
∩ ∩	3350	dusty rose, v. lt.
6 6	3609	plum, ultra lt.
= =	3685	mauve, dk.
m m	3687	mauve
e e	3688	mauve, lt.

Backstitch

⌐	white	*stars*
⌐	223	*sun, sun rays*
⌐	311	*borders around star-filled boxes, borders around large and small scenes, all lettering*
⌐	838	*child, quilt, sheets, pillow, dolls, birds*

French knot

•	311	*punctuation*
•	838	*birds' eyes, tips of clown-doll's mouth*

Satin stitch

⁄⁄⁄	838	*teddy bear's nose and eyes*

IF YOU ARE NOT HANDSOME

Shown on page 48

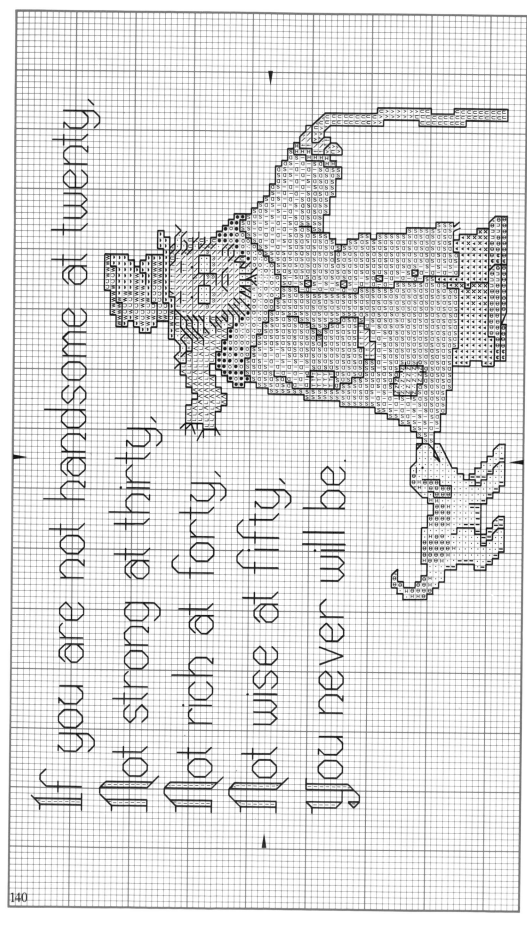

A perfect birthday sentiment for the husband with a good sense of humor! The original design was worked on aida 14 using 3 strands embroidery floss for cross-stitch and 2 strands for backstitch. Before starting, see *How Many Strands*, page 66.

Fabric	Design size	Fabric size for project shown
Aida 11	10¾″ × 7½″	17″ × 14″
Aida 14	8⅜″ × 5⅞″	14″ × 12″
Aida 18	6½″ × 4⅝″	13″ × 11″
Hardanger 22	5¾″ × 3¾″	12″ × 10″
Linen 32 (over 2)	7⅜″ × 5¼″	13″ × 11″

DMC Six-Strand Floss

Cross-stitch

· ·		white
⊤⊤	211	lavender, lt.
▲▲	315	antique mauve, dk.
××	316	antique mauve, med.
○○	352	coral, lt.
⊙⊙	353	peach flesh
●●	356	terra cotta, med.
ᴢᴢ	402	mahogany, v. lt.
◡◡	535	ash grey, v. lt.
ıı	543	beige-brown, ultra lt.
⌅⌅	632	rose brown, v. dk.
ᴡᴡ	647	beaver grey, med.
∧∧	676	old gold, lt.
ɪɪ	712	cream
ʟʟ	745	yellow, lt. pale
∖∖	754	peach flesh, lt.
⊤⊤	758	terra cotta, lt.
ᴠᴠ	841	beige-brown, lt.
ⴖⴖ	842	beige-brown, v. lt.
⊘⊘	930	antique blue, dk.
◌◌	931	antique blue, med.
⊤⊤	932	antique blue, lt.
∪∪	950	rose brown, lt.
◡◡	3024	brown-grey, v. lt.
⊕⊕	3064	rose brown, med.
∷∷	3706	melon, med.

Backstitch

⌐	838	*all*

French knot

•	838	*puppy, man, punctuation*

WEE WILLIE WINKIE

BOY'S ROOM SIGN • Shown on page 1

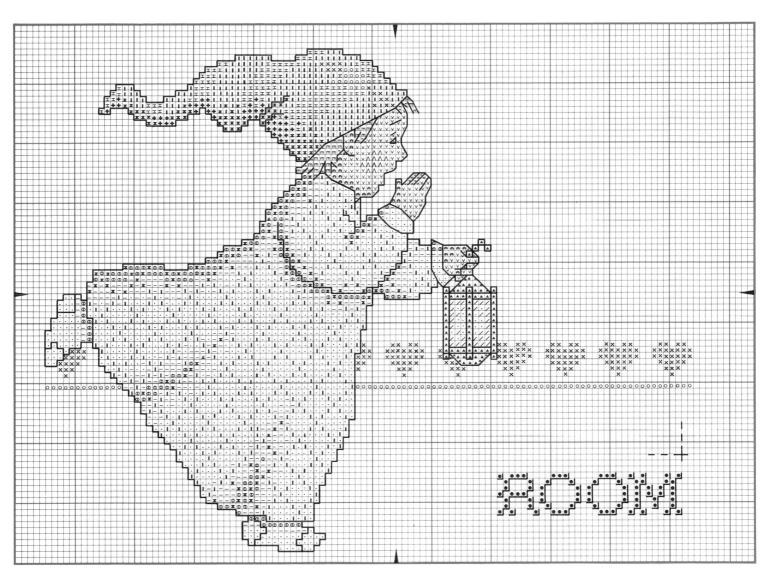

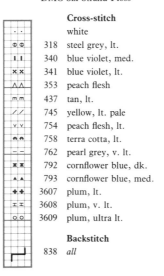

Wee Willie Winkie announces to the world that this bedroom belongs to your boy. You may choose, for a girl's room, to use the pattern on page 137.

The original design was worked using 2 strands embroidery floss for cross-stitch and 1 strand for back-stitch. To chart your child's name, see alphabets 6 and 8 on page 156, with the larger alphabet for the first letter of the name. Use medium blue violet (DMC 340) to cross-stitch the name and very dark beige-brown (DMC 838) to backstitch.

Fabric	Design size	Fabric size for project shown
Aida 14	6½″ × 8½″	12½″ × 14½″

DMC Six-Strand Floss

Cross-stitch		
· ·		white
⊕ ⊕	318	steel grey, lt.
I I	340	blue violet, med.
× ×	341	blue violet, lt.
∧ ∧	353	peach flesh
m m	437	tan, lt.
/ /	745	yellow, lt. pale
v v	754	peach flesh, lt.
ә ә	758	terra cotta, lt.
– –	762	pearl grey, v. lt.
⊠ ⊠	792	cornflower blue, dk.
▲ ▲	793	cornflower blue, med.
✦ ✦	3607	plum, lt.
⌶ ⌶	3608	plum, v. lt.
○ ○	3609	plum, ultra lt.
Backstitch		
⌐	838	*all*

WEE WILLIE WINKIE

Shown on page 51

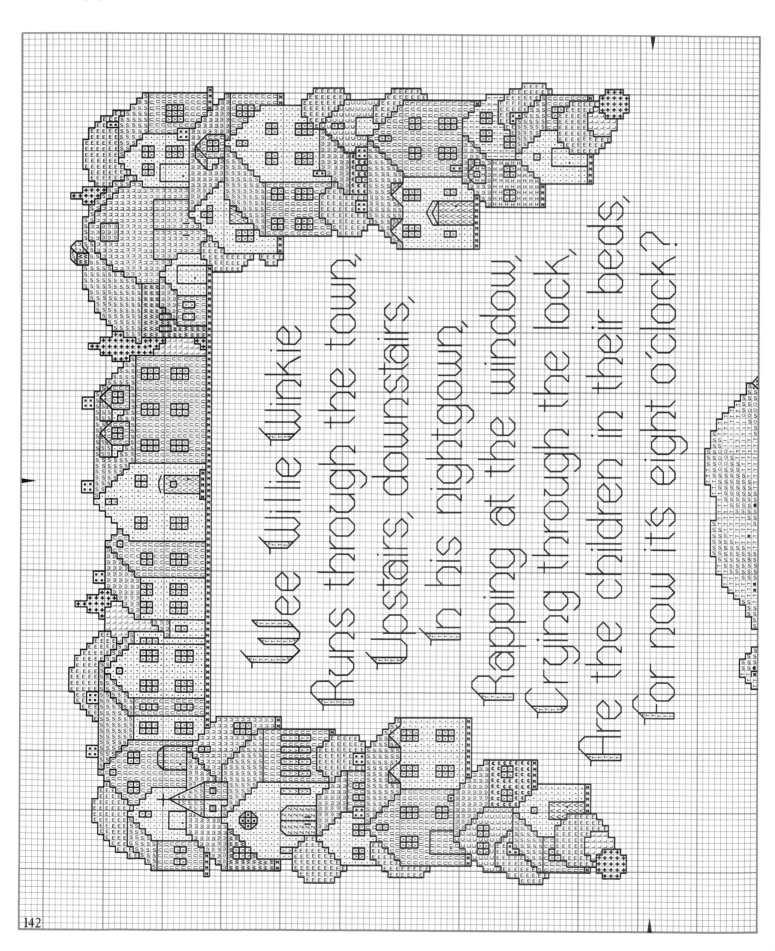

Parents and nursemaids throughout the centuries have always enlisted the aid of specialists to get their children to bed. If not Wee Willie Winkie or Winken, Blinken, and Nod, then perhaps the Sandman or the Slumber Wife. And if the children refused to be lulled to sleep, at least they could be kept in their beds by tales of the Bogie Man waiting in the closet.

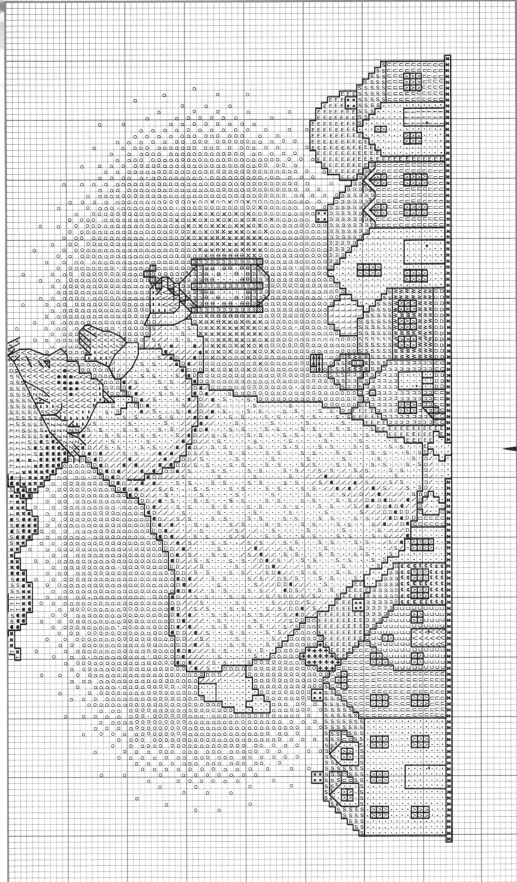

The original design was worked on aida 14 using 3 strands embroidery floss for cross-stitch and 2 strands for backstitch. Before starting, see *How Many Strands*, page 66.

A perfect accessory to the Wee Willie Winkie sampler is a personalized sign for your child's room. The pattern appears on page 141.

Fabric	Design size	Fabric size for project shown
Aida 11	12¼″ × 17¾″	19″ × 24″
Aida 14	9¾″ × 14″	16″ × 20″
Aida 18	7½″ × 10¾″	13½″ × 17″
Hardanger 22	6⅛″ × 8⅛″	12″ × 15″
Linen 32 (over 2)	8½″ × 12⅛″	14″ × 18″

DMC Six-Strand Floss

Cross-stitch

· ·		white
ɪ ɪ	210	lavender, med.
ł ł	211	lavender, lt.
ʊ ʊ	318	steel grey, lt.
▪ ▪	335	rose
s s	340	blue violet, med.
o o	341	blue violet, lt.
● ●	353	peach flesh
x x	414	steel grey, dk.
п п	415	pearl grey
z z	437	tan, lt.
L L	564	jade, v. lt.
c c	712	cream
v v	743	yellow, med.
x x	745	yellow, lt. pale
⊕ ⊕	746	off white
ʌ ʌ	754	peach flesh, lt.
▬ ▬	758	terra cotta, lt.
w w	760	salmon
u u	761	salmon, lt.
\ \	762	pearl grey, v. lt.
▪ ▪	792	cornflower blue, dk.
ω ω	793	cornflower blue, med.
ᴖ ᴖ	842	beige-brown, v. lt.
++ ++	992	aquamarine
m m	993	aquamarine, lt.
✕ ✕	3607	plum, lt.
ᴛ ᴛ	3608	plum, v. lt.
ɪ ɪ	3609	plum, ultra lt.

Backstitch

	white	*flag stripes (1 strand)*
	791	*nightshirt, nightcap, socks, lantern*
	792	*houses, trees, lettering*
	839	*face, hair, hands*

French knot

	792	*doorknobs, punctuation*

143

I SEE THE MOON

Shown on page 53

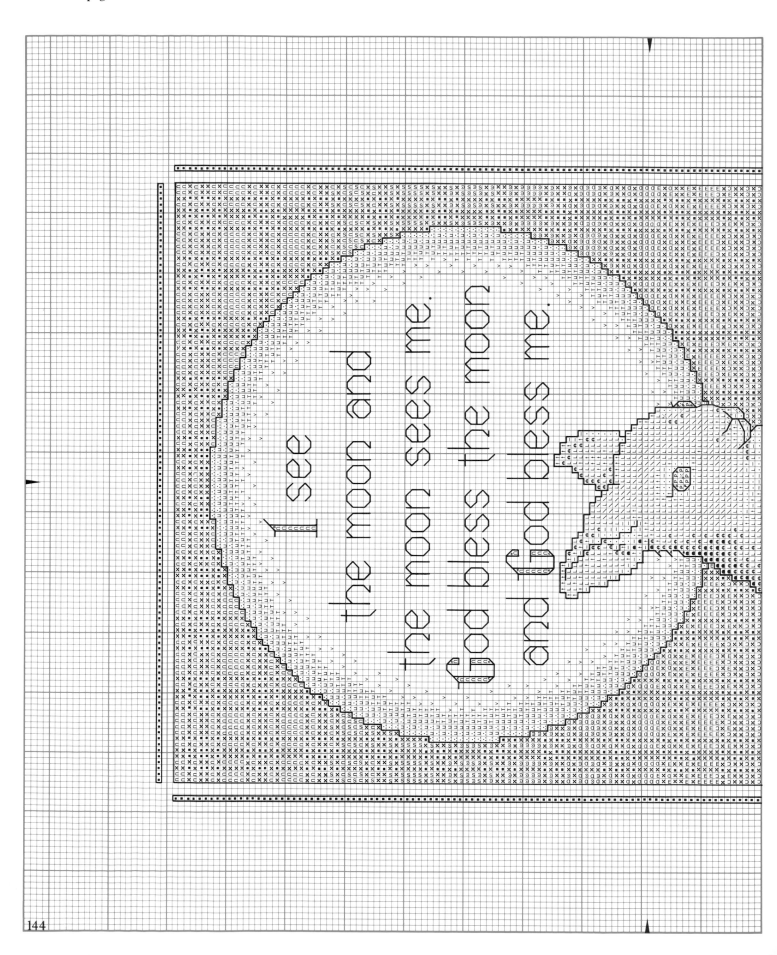

The simple sentiment in this lovely verse might once have been a charm to protect the nighttime traveler from moonlight, for it was widely believed the moon caused lunacy.

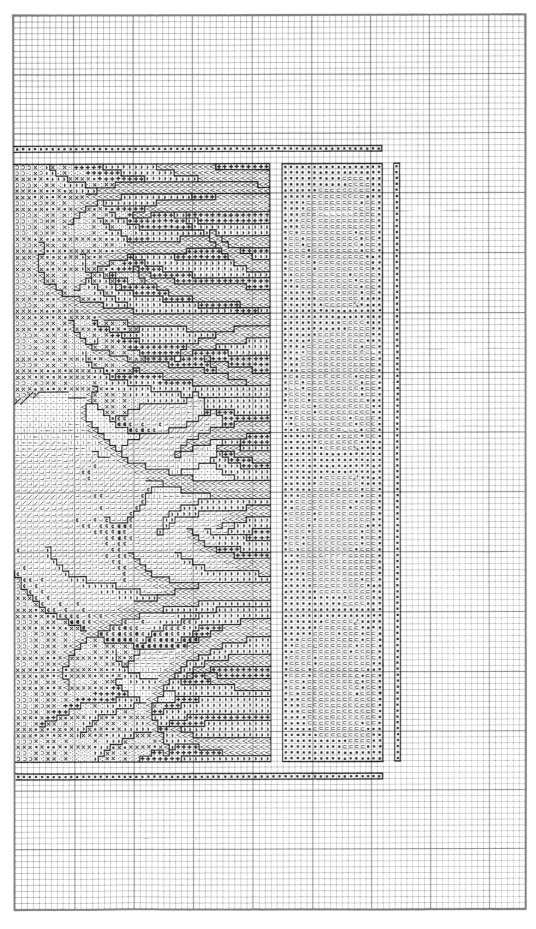

When working large areas, purchase all embroidery floss from the same dye-lot. To minimize flecks of fabric showing through, pull stitches uniformly taut, but not too tight.

The original design was worked on aida 14 using 3 strands embroidery floss for cross-stitch and 2 strands for backstitch. Before starting, see *How Many Strands,* page 66.

Fabric	Design size	Fabric size for project shown
Aida 11	9½″ × 15″	16″ × 21″
Aida 14	7¾″ × 11¾″	14″ × 18″
Aida 18	5⅞″ × 9¼″	12″ × 15″
Hardanger 22	4¾″ × 7½″	10″ × 13½″
Linen 32 (over 2)	6½″ × 10¼″	12″ × 16″

DMC Six-Strand Floss

Cross-stitch

· ·		white
ω ω	340	blue violet, med.
∴ ∴	353	peach flesh
P P	535	ash grey, v. lt.
↑ ↑	543	beige-brown, ultra lt.
ω ω	554	violet, lt.
∧ ∧	564	jade, v. lt.
▾ ▾	597	turquoise
– –	712	cream
u u	744	yellow, pale
т т	745	yellow, lt. pale
v v	746	off white
▪ ▪	792	cornflower blue, dk.
× ×	793	cornflower blue, med.
∩ ∩	794	cornflower blue, lt.
+ +	806	peacock blue, dk.
● ●	839	beige-brown, dk.
● ●	840	beige-brown, med.
L L	841	beige-brown, lt.
＼ ＼	842	beige-brown, v. lt.
m m	962	dusty rose, med.
◦ ◦	3688	mauve, med.
◡ ◡	3708	melon, lt.

Backstitch

⌐	838	*all*

French knot

•	838	*punctuation*

THE BOUGHS DO SHAKE

Shown on page 52

The original design was worked on aida 14 using 3 strands embroidery floss for cross-stitch and 2 strands for backstitch. Before starting, see *How Many Strands*, page 66.

Fabric	Design size	Fabric size for project shown
Aida 11	11¼" × 9"	17" × 15"
Aida 14	9" × 7⅛"	15" × 13"
Aida 18	7" × 5½"	13" × 11½"
Hardanger 22	5⅝" × 4½"	12" × 10½"
Linen 32 (over 2)	7⅞" × 6¼"	14" × 12"

DMC Six-Strand Floss

Cross-stitch

· ·		white
ı ı	347	salmon, dk.
m m	353	peach flesh
x x	413	pewter grey, dk.
s s	414	steel grey, dk.
L L	415	pearl grey
● ●	632	rose brown, v. dk.
ɪ ɪ	712	cream
n n	722	orange spice, lt.
+ +	743	yellow, med.
ᴗ ᴗ	745	yellow, lt. pale
\ \	754	peach flesh, lt.
x x	758	terra cotta, lt.
v v	760	salmon
ᴑ ᴑ	793	cornflower blue, med.
▲ ▲	921	copper
o o	945	rose brown
– –	948	peach flesh, v. lt.
▲ ▲	3064	rose brown, med.
ᴓ ᴓ	3328	salmon, med.

Backstitch

	838	*all*

French knot

•	838	*punctuation*

The boughs do shake,
The bells do ring,
So merrily comes
Our harvest in.

shake,

ing,

mes

CHILL DECEMBER

CHRISTMAS SERVING TRAY ﹅ Shown on page 64

The December Christmas wreath makes a cheerful holiday serving tray.

The design on the tray was worked on white aida 14 using 2 strands embroidery floss for cross-stitch and 1 strand for backstitch. The wooden tray shown has an oval opening of 9½" × 7".

Fabric	Design size	Fabric size for project shown
Aida 14	9½" × 7"	15½" × 13"

DMC Six-Strand Floss

Cross-stitch

I I	309	rose, deep
ʊ ʊ	320	pistachio green, med.
B B	321	christmas red
F F	369	pistachio green, v. lt.
+ +	501	blue-green, dk.
■ ■	816	garnet
K K	931	antique blue, med.
n n	932	antique blue, lt.
t t	962	dusty rose, med.

Backstitch

	814	*ribbon*
	924	*wreath, horizontal lines, lettering*

LITTLE JACK HORNER

Shown on page 56

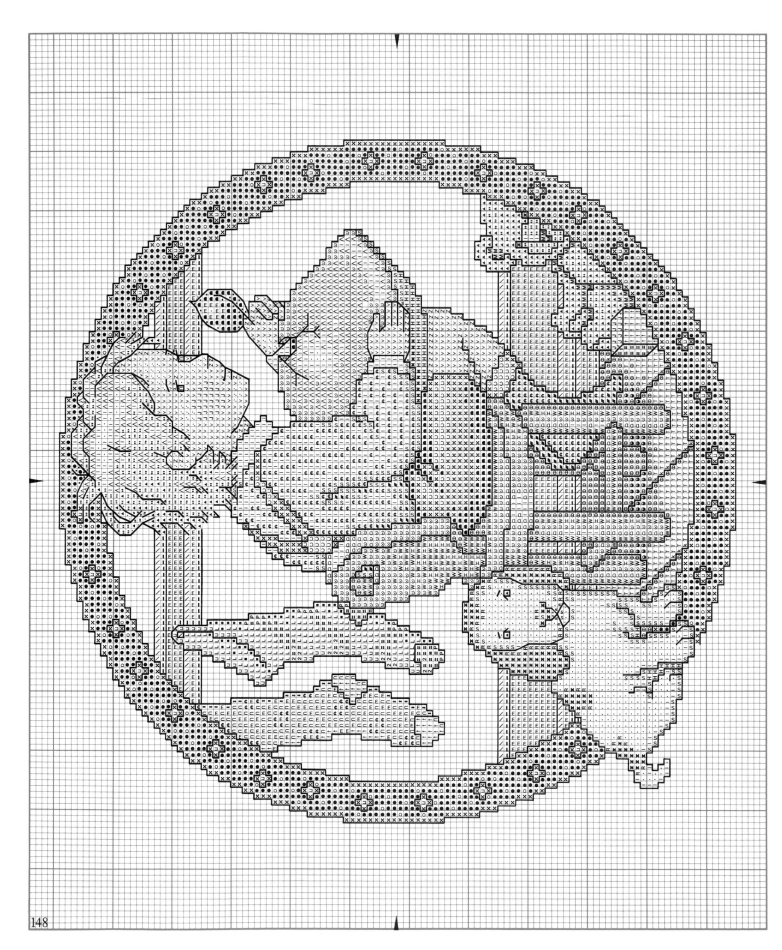

CHRISTMAS IS COMING

HOLLY CANDLE SCREEN ❧ Shown on page 64

Little Jack fits beautifully in a grapevine Christmas wreath (page 64). The original design was worked on aida 14 using 3 strands embroidery floss for cross-stitch and 2 strands for backstitch. Before starting, see *How Many Strands*, page 66.

Fabric	Design size	Fabric size for project shown
Aida 11	10½″ × 10½″	16½″ × 16½″
Aida 14	8¼″ × 8¼″	14″ × 14″
Aida 18	6⅜″ × 6⅜″	12½″ × 12½″
Hardanger 22	5¼″ × 5¼″	11″ × 11″
Linen 32 (over 2)	7¼″ × 7¼″	13″ × 13″

DMC Six-Strand Floss

Cross-stitch

		white
	223	shell pink, med.
m m	224	shell pink, lt.
\ \	225	shell pink, v. lt.
▲ ▲	315	antique mauve, dk.
■ ■	347	salmon, dk.
u u	352	coral, lt.
J J	353	peach flesh
T T	402	mahogany, v. lt.
▲ ▲	407	rose brown, dk.
w w	436	tan
◡ ◡	437	tan, lt.
● ●	501	blue-green, dk.
◢ ◢	502	blue-green
M M	632	rose brown, v. dk.
H H	645	beaver grey, v. dk.
R R	646	beaver grey, dk.
P P	676	old gold, lt.
ı ı	712	cream
◌ ◌	739	tan, ultra lt.
= =	744	yellow, pale
2 2	746	off white
v v	754	peach flesh, lt.
z z	758	terra cotta, lt.
◉ ◉	839	beige-brown, dk.
◍ ◍	840	beige-brown, med.
T T	841	beige-brown, lt.
k k	842	beige-brown, v. lt.
x x	844	beaver grey, ultra dk.
◌ ◌	899	rose, med.
ı ı	930	antique blue, dk.
n n	931	antique blue, med.
t t	932	antique blue, lt.
⁚ ⁚	948	peach flesh, v. lt.
ıı ıı	950	rose brown, lt.
∧ ∧	951	rose brown, v. lt.
⌒ ⌒	992	aquamarine
⌒ ⌒	993	aquamarine, lt.
H H	3022	brown-grey, med.
⌒ ⌒	3024	brown-grey, v. lt.
L L	3328	salmon, med.
x x	3350	dusty rose, v. dk.

Backstitch

	838	*all*

French knot

	838	*boy's mouth,*

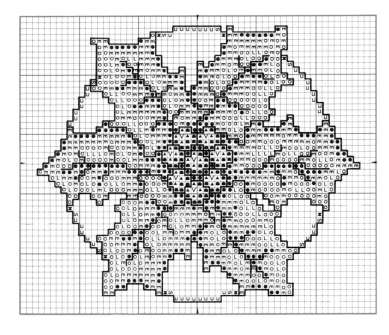

Accent a festive decor with holly candle screens. Then combine the candles with the holiday goose sampler and display your creative talents to the world. Candle screens are available through most needlework and craft shops.

The holly was worked on aida 14 using 2 strands embroidery floss for cross-stitch and 1 strand for backstitch.

Fabric	Design size	Fabric size for project shown
Aida 14	4″ × 4″	9″ × 9″

DMC Six-Strand Floss

Cross-stitch

m m	320	pistachio green, med.
▲ ▲	321	christmas red
◌ ◌	368	pistachio green, lt.
L L	369	pistachio green, v. lt.
● ●	501	blue-green, dk.
⌒ ⌒	725	topaz
u u	744	yellow, pale
x x	783	christmas gold
◢ ◢	816	garnet
v v	963	dusty rose, v. lt.

Backstitch

	500	*leaves*
	838	*berries*
	840	*gold ring*

Ancient tales claim that a goose, symbol of watchfulness, first greeted the Three Wise Men when they arrived at the stable in Bethlehem.

The original design was worked on aida 14 using 3 strands embroidery floss for cross-stitch and 2 strands for backstitch. Before starting, see *How Many Strands*, page 66.

As an accessory to the Christmas goose, a holly spray was designed (pattern, page 149) to be displayed in the candle screen.

Fabric	Design size	Fabric size for project shown
Aida 11	13¼″ × 18″	19″ × 24″
Aida 14	10⅜″ × 14⅜″	16½″ × 20″
Aida 18	8″ × 11″	14″ × 17″
Hardanger 22	6½″ × 9⅛″	12½″ × 15″
Linen 32 (over 2)	9″ × 12½″	15″ × 18″

DMC Six-Strand Floss

Cross-stitch

· ·		white
● ●	301	mahogany, med.
I I	309	rose, deep
+ +	320	pistachio green, med.
○ ○	321	christmas red
s s	368	pistachio green, lt.
- -	369	pistachio green, v. lt.
R R	402	mahogany, v. lt.
■ ■	501	blue-green, dk.
m m	503	blue-green, mcd.
L L	543	beige-brown, ultra lt.
\ \	712	cream
u u	725	topaz
∧ ∧	744	yellow, pale
3 3	746	off white
○ ○	778	antique mauve, lt.
■ ■	782	topaz, med.
N N	783	christmas gold
x x	816	garnet
● ●	841	beige-brown, lt.
○ ○	842	beige-brown, v. lt.
= =	922	copper, lt.
⌄ ⌄	926	grey-green, dk.
w w	930	antique blue, dk.
z z	931	antique blue, med.
x x	932	antique blue, lt.
◖ ◖	961	dusty rose, dk.
○ ○	962	dusty rose, med.
t t	963	dusty rose, v. lt.
▲ ▲	3041	antique violet, med.
∩ ∩	3687	mauve
∩ ∩	3688	mauve, med.
T T	3689	mauve, lt.

Backstitch

	500	*large C, lettering, holly leaves*
	814	*ribbon around goose's neck*
	838	*goose, holly berries*
	840	*ribbons spiraling vertically on left and right side*
	924	*trees, green border*
	931	*checkerboard behind goose*

French knot

·	500	*punctuation*

GOLDEN SLUMBERS

Shown on page 57

Nursery rhymes don't always stay in the nursery. Dinah Shore's 1948 hit "Lavender Blue" was a popular dance tune on both sides of the Atlantic. And The Beatles sang their own, slightly lengthened version of "Golden Slumbers."

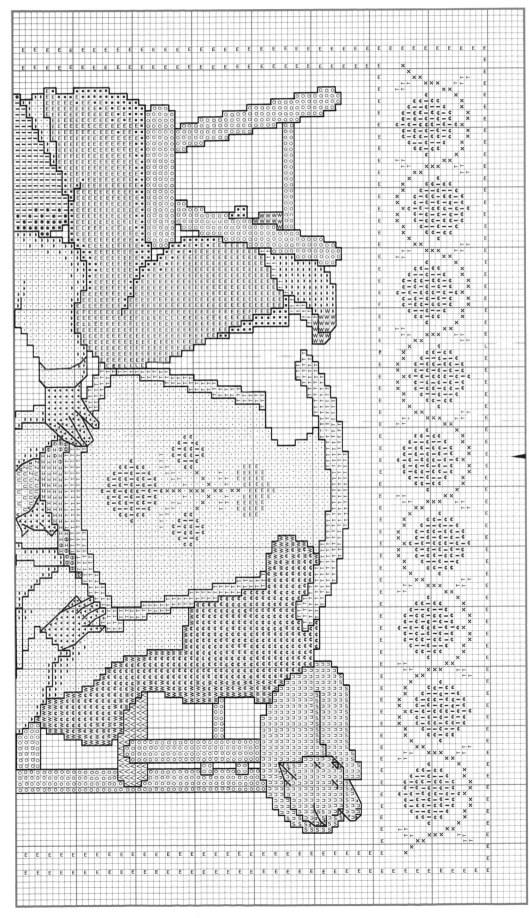

When embroidering hands and faces, in order to create greater realism and expression, the backstitch line does not always run from corner to corner in the grid. Follow the chart carefully.

The original design was worked on aida 14 using 3 strands embroidery floss for cross-stitch and 2 strands for backstitch. Before starting, see *How Many Strands*, page 66.

Fabric	Design size	Fabric size for project shown
Aida 11	12¾″ × 18″	19″ × 24″
Aida 14	10″ × 14⅜″	16″ × 20″
Aida 18	7¾″ × 11″	14″ × 17″
Hardanger 22	6⅜″ × 9⅛″	12″ × 15″
Linen 32 (over 2)	8¾″ × 12½″	15″ × 18″

DMC Six-Strand Floss

Cross-stitch

· ·		white
l l	316	antique mauve, med.
l l	318	steel grey, lt.
+ +	353	peach flesh
⊠ ⊠	414	steel grey, dk.
◡ ◡	415	pearl grey
z z	436	tan
× ×	598	turquoise, lt.
◖◗	676	old gold, lt.
u u	712	cream
n n	738	tan, v. lt.
ᴗ ᴗ	739	tan, ultra lt.
⊖ ⊖	744	yellow, pale
▲ ▲	754	peach flesh, lt.
w w	760	salmon
⊝ ⊝	761	salmon, lt.
■ ■	793	cornflower blue, med.
m m	794	cornflower blue, lt.
v v	841	beige-brown, lt.
∧ ∧	945	rose brown
T T	966	baby green, med.
● ●	3041	antique violet, med.
o o	3064	rose brown, med.
I I	3078	golden yellow, v. lt.
◡ ◡	3328	salmon, med.

Backstitch

⌐	839	*all*

French knot

•	839	*eyes, punctuation*

OF ALL THE SAYINGS

Shown on page 58

Needle position

GOLDEN SLUMBERS

NURSERY DOOR SASH ▪ Shown on page 1

The original design was worked on aida 14 using 3 strands embroidery floss for cross-stitch and 2 strands for backstitch. Use 1 strand backstitch for the loop of thread. Before starting, see *How Many Strands*, page 66.

Complete the work by inserting a rustproof needle where indicated.

Fabric	Design size	Fabric size for project shown
Aida 11	8¼″ × 10½″	14″ × 16½″
Aida 14	6½″ × 8¼″	12½″ × 14″
Linen 32 (over 2)	5⅝″ × 7¼″	11½″ × 13″

Cross-stitch

· ·		white
V V	210	lavender, med.
u u	353	peach flesh
t t	776	pink, med.
m m	930	antique blue, dk.
c c	3609	plum, ultra lt.

Backstitch

	930	*lettering, flower stems, loops of thread*

French knot

·	930	*punctuation*

"Sh-h-h-h" reads the notice on the nursery door. Once those golden slumbers have begun, no one wants to wake baby. The sash was worked on aida 14 using 2 strands embroidery floss for cross-stitch and 1 strand for backstitch.

Fabric	Design size	Fabric size for project shown
Aida 14	4⅝″ × 6⅛″	10″ × 12″
Linen 32 (over 2)	4⅛″ × 5¼″	10″ × 12″

DMC Six-Strand Floss

Cross-stitch

· ·		white
I I	316	antique mauve, med.
∾ ∾	415	pearl grey
z z	436	tan
x x	598	turquoise, lt.
∩ ∩	738	tan, v. lt.
⊖ ⊖	744	yellow, pale
▲ ▲	754	peach flesh, lt.
∩ ∩	761	salmon, lt.
m m	794	cornflower blue, lt.
T T	966	baby green, med.
I I	3078	golden yellow, v. lt

Backstitch

	839	*all*

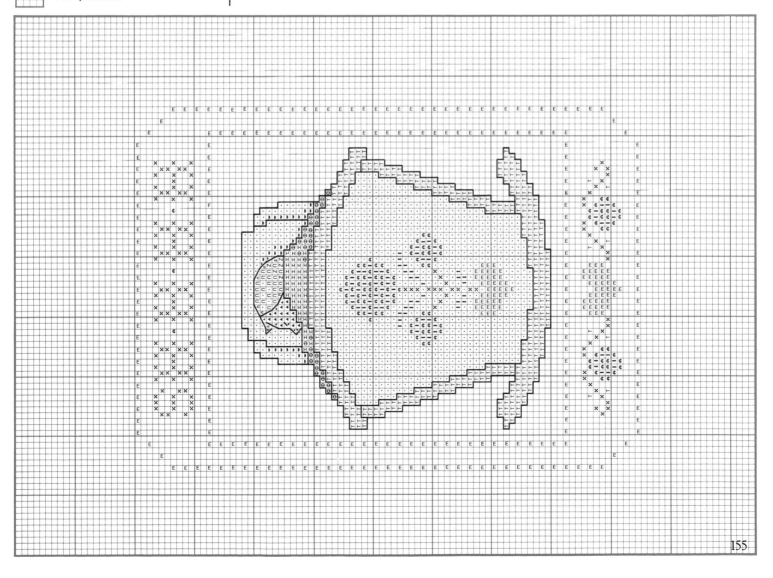

BIBLIOGRAPHY

ALLEN, GLORIA SEAMAN. *Family Record: Genealogical Watercolors and Needlework*. Washington, D.C.: DAR Museum, 1989.

BARING-GOULD, WILLIAM S. and CEIL. *The Annotated Mother Goose*. New York: Clarkson N. Potter, 1962.

BOLTON, ETHEL STANWOOD and EVA JOHNSON COE. *American Samplers*. Boston: Massachusetts Society of the Colonial Dames of America, 1921.

CLABBURN, PAMELA. *The Needleworker's Dictionary*. London: Macmillan, 1976.

DON, SARAH. *Traditional Samplers*. New York: Viking, 1986.

FORIS, MARIA and ANDREAS. *Charted Folk Designs for Cross-stitch Embroidery*, trans. Heinz Edgar Kiewe. New York: Dover Publications, 1975.

HARBESON, GEORGIANA BROWN. *American Needlework*. New York: Coward-McCann, 1938.

HUISH, MARCUS. *Samplers and Tapestry Embroideries*, 2nd ed. London: Longmans, Green, 1913.

HURLIMANN, BETTINA. *Three Centuries of Children's Books in Europe*, trans. Brian W. Alderson. London: Oxford University Press, 1967.

KASSELL, HILDA. *Stitches in Time*. New York: Duell, Sloan and Pearce, 1966.

KRUEGER, GLEE. *A Gallery of American Samplers: The Theodore H. Kapnek Collection*. New York: E.P. Dutton, 1978.

———. *New England Samplers to 1840*. Sturbridge, Mass.: Old Sturbridge Village, 1978.

LEE, KAY and MARSHALL. *Book of Days*. New York: G.P. Putnam's Sons, 1979.

OPIE, IONA and PETER. *The Oxford Book of Nursery Rhymes*. New York: Oxford University Press, 1951.

POLLY, JANE, ed. *American Folklore and Legend*. Pleasantville, N.Y./ Montreal: The Reader's Digest Association, 1978.

RING, BETTY. *American Needlework Treasures*. New York: E.P. Dutton, 1987.

———. "The Balch School in Providence, Rhode Island," *Antiques*. Apr., 1975.

———. "Mary Balch's Newport Sampler," *Antiques*. Sept., 1983.

———. *Needlework—An Historical Survey*. New York: Universe Books, Antiques Magazine Library, 1975.

———. "Salem Female Academy," *Antiques*. Sept., 1974.

———. "Samplers and Silk Embroideries of Portland, Maine," *Antiques*. Sept., 1988.

SAWYER, MARY and her Neighbors and Friends. *The Story of Mary's Little Lamb*. Published by Mr. and Mrs. Henry Ford, 1928. Sudbury, Mass.: Facsimile edition by Longfellow's Wayside Inn.

SCHIFFER, MARGARET B. *Historical Needlework of Pennsylvania*. New York: Charles Scribner's Sons, 1958.

SEBBA, ANNE. *Samplers, Five Centuries of a Gentle Craft*. New York: Thames & Hudson, 1979.

STUDEBAKER, SUE. *Ohio Samplers: Schoolgirl Embroideries, 1803–1850*. Lebanon, Ohio: Warren County Historical Society, 1988.

SWAN, SUSAN BURROWS. *Winterthur Guide to American Needlework*. New York: Crown Publishers, Rutledge Books, 1976.

The True Mother Goose. New York and Boston: C.S. Francis and Co., 1833; Facsimile edition by Merrimack Publishing.

WEISSMAN, JUDITH REITER and WENDY LAVITT. *Labors of Love: America's Textiles and Needlework, 1650–1930*. New York: Alfred A. Knopf, 1987.

NEEDLEWORK CREDITS

Ursula M. Paccone, front cover; Pam Grant, endpapers and pg. 15; Carol Arnold, pgs. 7, 13, 44; Pat Batulis, pg. 8; Geraldine Schultz, pgs. 9, 23, 29, 41; Debra Haldeman, pgs. 10, 35; Vicki I. Bennett, pgs. 11, 50; Frances Padgett, pgs. 12, 56; Judy Clark, pg. 14; Nancy A. Doman, pg. 16; Victoria Rounds, pgs. 17, 31; Debbie A. Jacobus, pg. 18; Sharon J. Newman, pgs. 19, 36, 48; Ruth Elizabeth Bruning, pgs. 20, 51; Lisa Hilliard, pg. 21; Laura L. Palmer, pg. 22; Cathy Clark Harrell, pg. 24; Kay Leininger, pg. 25; Margaret Brennan, pg. 26; Reges J. Bush, pg. 27; Bob Schultz, pg. 28; Patricia M. Bottcher, pg. 30; Mary Jane Buchanan, pgs. 32, 33, 40; Carolyn S. Winslow, pg. 34; Nancy H. Paddock, pg. 37; Mary Jane Rolls, pg. 38; Marcia H. Robinson, pg. 39; Cheri A. McElroy, pg. 42; Debbie Reynolds, pg. 43; Patricia Reimsnyder, pg. 45; Jennifer T. Long, pg. 46; Deborah M. Spezialetti, pg. 47; Denise K. Hagan, pg. 49; Jackie Yacubic, pg. 52; Maria D. Russ, pg. 53; Mary E. Hildreth, pg. 54; Kelly Pickering, pg. 55; Sandra A. Clemons, pg. 57; Susan H. Arnold, pg. 58.

Needlework appearing in still-life photos: Nettie Caporiccio; Marie K. Dale; Janet I. Pierotti; Anne E. Marshall; Judith D. Gulick; Jane Sugawara; Eileen Warren; Ann-Marie Allaire; Eileen N. Hogan; W. Richard Hamlin, Ph. D.; Susannah K. Murphy; Maria D. Russ; Denise K. Hagan; Frances Padgett; Cheri A. McElroy; Kelly Pickering; Geraldine Schultz; Ruth Elizabeth Bruning; Nancy H. Paddock; Debra Haldeman; and Carol Arnold.

INDEX OF NEEDLEWORK
AND PATTERNS

	Needlework	Pattern		*Needlework*	Pattern
Garden Arch	2	68	Little Drops of Water	34	116
My Melodies	7	69	I Like Little Pussy	35	—
January Brings the Snow	8	—	Pussycat, Pussycat	35	118
The North Wind Doth Blow	8	70–71	There Was Once a Fish	36	122
Whether It's Cold	9	72–73	Rainbow in the West	36	—
The Greedy Man	9	—	Jack and Jill	37	120–121
I Saw Three Ships	10	—	August Brings the Sheaves of Corn	38	—
How Many Days	11	74–75	All Work and No Play	38	123
Teddy Bear	11	77	If You Are to Be a Gentleman	39	124–125
February Brings the Rain	12	—	Calico Pie	40	—
Lavender Blue	12	76	Charley Warley	40	—
The Rose Is Red	13	78–79	Sleep, Baby, Sleep	41	126–127
Yankee Doodle	14	80–81	September Offers	42	—
When Jack's a Very Good Boy	14	—	Cornucopia	42	135
Hey Diddle, Diddle	15	82–83	A Neat Little Clock	42	130–131
March Brings Breezes	16	—	Mary Had a Little Lamb	43	128–129
One Leaf for Fame	16	84	Detail	1	130
Sing a Song of Sixpence	17	86–87	Monday's Child	44	—
There Was a Crooked Man	18	—	I Had a Little Hobby Horse	44	134–135
Welcome Sign	64	88	Great A, Little a	45	132–133
See a Pin	18	89	Fresh October Brings the Pheasant	46	—
Daffy-Down-Dilly	19	90–91	Make Your Candles Last	46	—
April Brings the Primrose	20	—	Girl's Room Sign	1	137
I Bought a Dozen New-Laid Eggs	20	97–98	Tommy's Tears and Mary's Fears	47	—
Rain, Rain, Go Away	21	92–93	Three Little Ghostesses	47	136–137
Baby and I	22	—	Catch Him, Crow	48	—
Cackle, Cackle	22	98–99	If You Are Not Handsome	48	140
One, Two, Buckle My Shoe	23	94–95	Good Night, Sleep Tight	49	138–139
May Brings Flocks	24	—	Dull November Brings the Blast	50	—
Lamb Bib	1	85	A Wise Old Owl	50	—
One, He Loves	24	96	Wee Willie Winkie	51	142–143
May Flowers	25	100–101	Boy's Room Sign	1	141
The Cock Crows	26	104–105	The Boughs Do Shake	52	146
Pat-a-Cake	26	—	Ride Away, Ride Away	52	—
The Fair Maid	27	102–103	I See the Moon	53	144–145
June Brings Tulips	28	—	Chill December	54	—
Sachet Bag	1	117	Christmas Serving Tray	64	147
Birds of a Feather	28	105	Smiling Girls, Rosy Boys	54	—
Hearts Like Doors	29	106–107	Christmas Is Coming	55	150–151
Table Set	64	106–108	Holly Candle Screen	64	149
Good, Better, Best	30	109	When December Snows Fall Fast	56	—
Jenny Wren	30	—	Little Jack Horner	56	148
Mary Mary, Quite Contrary	31	110–111	Golden Slumbers	57	152–153
Winter, Spring, Summer, Autumn	32–33	112–115	Nursery Door Sash	1	155
Hot July	34	—	Of All the Sayings	58	154
Fruit Basket	1	119			

More than fifty people contributed their time and expertise to *Mother Goose's Words of Wit and Wisdom*. The work in this volume has been designed, stitched, and charted with painstaking care. Nevertheless, there exists the possibility of human, mechanical, or printing error and the variability of personal stitching styles. We cannot be held responsible for such errors though we invite any queries and comments to be mailed to the address below.

Limited space prevents the inclusion of a few patterns to some of the stitcheries appearing in this book. If you desire one of these patterns (cover not available), please send $1.00 and a self-addressed, stamped #10 envelope to:

Mother Goose's Words
P.O. Box 4363
Elmira, NY 14904